CAROBLEAT'S COFFIN WAS SCARCELY COLD . . .

when his next-door neighbor required another. Marcus Gwill had been found at the foot of an electrical tower with a mouthful of marshmallows. And Inspector Purbright had never known a suicide with a sweet tooth.

Two deaths in six months raised more than a few puzzling questions. And the ingenious inspector was determined to find the answers —even if it made him a candidate for the next Flaxborough funeral . . . the next target in a diabolical scheme of blackmail and murder.

Murder Ink.® Mysteries

Scene Of The Crime™ Mysteries

A Murder Ink.® Mystery

COFFIN SCARCELY USED

Colin Watson

A DELL BOOK

Published by
Dell Publishing Co., Inc.
1 Dag Hammarskjold Plaza
New York, New York 10017

Dell ® TM 681510, Dell Publishing Co., Inc.

ISBN: 0-440-11511-6

Reprinted by arrangement with the author
Printed in the United States of America
First Dell printing—October 1981

COFFIN
SCARCELY
USED

CHAPTER ONE

Considering that Mr Harold Carobleat had been in his time a town councillor of Flaxborough, a justice of the peace, a committeeman of the Unionist Club, and, reputedly, the owner of the town's first television aerial, his funeral was an uninspiring affair.

And considering the undoubted prosperity of Mr Carobleat's business establishment, the ship brokerage firm of Carobleat and Spades, its closing almost simultaneously with the descent of its owner's coffin into a hole in Heston Lane Cemetery was but another sign that *gloria mundi* transits as hastily in Flaxborough as anywhere else.

There were those, of course, who were pleased to interpret both circumstances otherwise than philosophically. They hoped for scandal, even posthumous scandal, to compensate for what had been, by their standards, a singularly uneventful burying and the tantalizingly straightforward eclipse of a well-known local business. They were in no mood to accept the explanation that a firm with only one principal (Mr Spades was a fiction that derived from some good-will arrangement made by Mr Carobleat when he took over the concern in 1935) could reasonably be expected to share his demise.

But, then, uncharitable speculation was no novelty in Flaxborough. It flecked the canvas of community life and, like the blemish that invites anxious exam-

ination of an old master, made it the more interesting.

What was wrong with the funeral?

Well, for one thing, there were only three cars. Not
that there really needed to be any at all. The tall,
sombre-faced house, standing behind its looming
hedges at the far end of the built-up portion of Heston Lane, was little more than fifty yards from the
cemetery entrance. But that wasn't the point. Even
had the grave yawned in the middle of Mr Carobleat's own front lawn, propriety would have demanded a cortege of Daimlers to go once round the
drive before unloading at the point from which it
had set out.

No, three cars meant that the austerity suggested in
the *Flaxborough Citizen* announcement of 'funeral
private; friends meet at cemetery' had been deliberately put into effect. The town, conscious of its enti-
tlement to make the best of the only genuine
'engagement elsewhere' that had ever kept Mr Carobleat from serving its interests, felt snubbed. It
resented such flagrant unostentation.

There was no service at either church or chapel.
Nor was there held that funeral equivalent to a
wedding reception, the nameless function designed to
thaw out the feet of mourning and to enable grief to
be beguiled with a few preliminary guesses about the
will.

At the end of what brief, colourless ceremony there
had been at the graveside, the few representatives of
the council and one or two other organizations with
which Harold Carobleat had been associated each
solemnly grasped the black-gloved hand of Joan Carobleat, relict, murmured a kindly encouragement and
departed. Mrs Carobleat's face remained expression-
less but she thanked them quietly one by one. When
all had passed, she turned and awaited Mr Jonas

Bradlaw, undertaker, who personally drove her home in the second car.

The subsequent cold meal was served only to a few of the former broker's closest friends. There was his medical adviser (if 'adviser' remains an appropriate term on such an occasion), Dr Rupert Hillyard; Mr Rodney Gloss, his solicitor; Mr Marcus Gwill, proprietor of the *Flaxborough Citizen* and the Carobleats' next-door neighbour; and Mr Bradlaw—for even amongst one's friends one may number those of whose professional services one does not wish to take immediate advantage, at whatever discount.

No relatives arrived to sour the occasion, for the Carobleat family tree had been so effectively pruned by childless marriage, chronic spinsterism, ill choice of occupation in two wars, and an hereditary susceptibility to heart disease that Harold had been for some time the last twig on the dead trunk of his ancestry.

The only outsider to be entertained was a young reporter from the *Citizen*, and he was quietly taken into an alcove by Mr Gwill and given by him a succinct biography and a list of mourners. There had been, by request, no flowers.

So passed from Flaxborough a man who, in Mr Gwill's carefully chosen phrases, had been 'a respected citizen of the town since he took up residence twenty-two years ago and applied himself to the expansion of a long-established local business; a notable social worker, particularly in the sphere of moral welfare as it affected the good name of our small maritime community; and an administrator who will long be remembered for his contribution to the organizing of the war effort in this area.'

As the blinds of the tall, withdrawn Edwardian villas on Heston Lane were released from the tension of indicating begrudged respect for Three-Car Carobleat, a police inspector strolled, apparently aimlessly, past the gates of Karachi, the homestead so lately vacated by Harold. Having noticed that Mr Bradlaw's second Daimler was still on the drive, he sauntered on a little way and eventually took a bus back to the town. The following day, he reasoned, would be a more seemly occasion for a tactful, informal talk with Mrs Carobleat. And, indeed, the inspector did call the next day. But he learned nothing to his purpose.

It was a little more than six months later that the good residents of Heston Lane found themselves constrained to darken their front rooms once again.

This time, however, the occasion was one of much more intriguing possibilities. Who would have thought that one of the mourners at Mr Carobleat's funeral in May would take a December journey in the same direction—and from the very next house, too? And what was one to make of the curious circumstances of this new death?

The same question was occupying the mind of the reporter who had stood respectfully in the big, expensively furnished drawing-room of Karachi, matching his shorthand against Mr Gwill's recital of Harold Carobleat's civic career.

This reporter now sat at his desk in the barn-like office above the clattering case-room, and wondered what sort of an obituary one composed in respect of one's own employer. Judging from the lavish record of every public word and act of Mr Gwill that the *Citizen* had been obliged to print in his lifetime, it seemed that the announcement of the catastrophe of his death called for the efforts of Aeschylus, Jonson, Wordsworth and Barnum and Bailey, all rolled into one.

Yet how could heroic prose ('. . . the entire community, deeply shocked and tragically aware of the loss it has sustained . . .') be bent to make room for factual details so bizarre as those of the accident in Callendar's Field?

He stared impotently at the blank copy paper before him and received only the mental image of Mr Marcus Gwill, his pale blue eyes like ice fragments beneath the unsympathetic cliff of his forehead, gazing coldly across Flaxborough from the extraordinary vantage point of the crossbar of an electricity pylon.

Across the narrow corridor from the general editorial office where inspiration eluded the epitaph-writer was a smaller, warmer and much, much more comfortable room. Behind its heavy mahogany table sat a sharply featured man with busy, distrustful eyes and a wide slit of a mouth, designed, one would have thought, for the dual purpose of loud talk and voracious feeding.

In fact, however, Mr George Lintz, editor of the *Flaxborough Citizen*, made miserly use of his most extravagant feature, for he ate little and spoke only one-sidedly, as though half his lips had been sewn up to prevent waste of words and body heat.

On this misty, yellowish winter morning, Lintz was staring fixedly ahead through one of the three tall windows that faced him. He lightly held the telephone with the mouthpiece down under his chin in the manner of the newspaper man. He remained silently attentive for a full minute, then, in sudden exasperation, barked 'Nonsense!' and shifted forward in his chair.

'You can get that idea out of your head straight away,' he said, speaking now directly into the receiver. 'There's nothing in or near the house that can possibly hurt you. You can't simply . . .' He paused and listened impatiently to some further objection, interrupting with 'No, of course, I don't know why he went out. I wasn't there. Nor were you. If you listen to every silly tale from weak-witted farm labourers, you'll end up by seeing a vampire or something every time you look out of a window. All we know is that my uncle did a damn silly trick at a damn silly time and got himself killed. People do get taken that way, God knows why. They go running under buses or fall off towers or jump into rivers. But that doesn't mean they've been chased or pushed by the supernatural. The best thing you can do, Mrs Poole, is to make yourself a strong cup of tea and forget all about it until I get over this evening.'

'Heaven save me,' said Lintz, leaning forward and replacing the telephone, 'from housekeepers who have horrid presentiments.'

'They can be rather trying, sir.'

This expression of sympathy came from a dark corner of the room where a large, but unassuming-looking man in neutral shaded clothes had been keeping quite still during the editor's telephone conversation. He now turned into the light and revealed a bland, pleasant face beneath springy, corn-coloured hair that not even relentless cropping could bring to conformity.

'I once had a landlady,' he remarked, 'who tried to stop me going on duty because she'd dreamed of a policeman lying in a pool of blood at the end of Coronation Street. She was always having this damned dream, d'you know, and it wasn't until a bus conductor cut his throat somewhere round that district that she stopped pestering me and admitted she might have been mistaken about the uniform.'

Detective Inspector Purbright regarded Lintz affably. 'I gather,' he said, 'that you discount the idea of the lady you were speaking to just now that your uncle was—how did she put it?—lured or chased out of his house?'

'I think she was just being stupid. Or hysterical.'

'Yes. Now that's very probable. A highly strung lady, perhaps?'

'Imaginative, but not very intelligent. I believe she dabbles in spiritualism.' Lintz, a lay preacher among other things, evidently considered Mrs Poole's interest in the occult a grave detraction from her reliability as a witness to anything but trumpets and cheesecloth.

'Tell me, Mr Lintz, Mr Gwill didn't happen to have any ideas of that kind himself, did he?'

'Lord, no. He was very down to earth. If you see what I mean,' added Lintz hastily.

'I see, sir. A level-headed man. But maybe not so materialistically minded, you understand, that he would do nothing out of the normal run occasionally?'

The editor looked puzzled. Purbright made a little gesture of good-natured humility and smiled. 'I put things rather awkwardly, don't I? What I am looking for, d'you know, is an explanation of why your uncle went out last night. He fancied a little walk, do you imagine?'

'What, in his slippers?'

'Yes, that is curious, isn't it? If I had occasion to walk down the drive of that house and cross the road and then climb a railing and go twenty yards over a field before clambering up an electricity pylon, I really believe I'd put my boots on first.' Purbright stared at his toe-caps.

Lintz offered no comment. He looked round at the clock on the wall to his left. 'Coffee?' he asked. Assured that that would be most kind of him, he gave an order to the girl on the switchboard, then pushed a box of cigarettes across the table to the inspector.

Until the girl's arrival with a tray, Purbright said no more about Uncle Marcus but kept the conversation offshore, as it were. Then, apologetically, he veered back to the subject of electrocution.

'Do you know, sir, that your uncle's is the first case of an accident with those cables since the power was brought over in the twenties? Or so the Board tells me. He's been a singularly unfortunate gentleman.'

Lintz shrugged and spooned sugar into his coffee. 'Have you any ideas about it, inspector?'

'I really don't think I have, sir. As time goes on, things may become a little clearer, but I wouldn't presume to speculate before hearing more about Mr Gwill from people who knew him. Mrs Poole, now. Do you think she might help me to get a better picture?'

'Mrs Poole would waste your time,' said the editor, decisively. 'Wouldn't it be better if we faced at once the probability of my uncle having chosen an odd but effective way of committing suicide?'

Purbright raised an eyebrow. 'You think that, sir?'

'My dear chap, what else is there to think? He wasn't a child or an idiot. And a grown man in his right mind doesn't climb pylons in the middle of the night just to feel if the current's still on.'

'I have known gentleman do rather eccentric things when the mood took them.'

'My uncle was not an eccentric. He managed to make too much money for that.'

'I suppose you'll have no cause to regret his good business sense.' Purbright caught Lintz's quick glance and added, 'A newspaper is like any other concern, I expect—easier to take over when it's running well.'

'That seems logical.'

There was a short pause.

'Talking of businesses,' said Purbright, 'I seem to

remember that that man with the unlikely name used to live near Mr Gwill. The broker chap. . . .'

'Carobleat?'

'That's the one. He died not so long ago.'

'Carobleat lived next door to my uncle. His wife's still there . . . widow, rather.'

'Is she really? You'd think a big house like that would be rather overwhelming. I must call and see how she's coping when I go over later on.'

'You're going to my uncle's place?'

'Oh, yes. I think I ought to take a quick look, don't you? The people round there are mostly timid old souls. An unhappy affair like this tends to prey on their minds a little, and they feel better when they see a policeman turn up. I find they regard me as a sort of exorcist.'

'Mrs Poole won't, I warn you. Not unless you take a stake with you and promise you're looking for a likely corpse to immobilize with it.'

Purbright beamed and rose. 'You're a sensible man, Mr Lintz. I'm glad to see you taking this unfortunate affair so well.'

He shook hands and was almost out of the door when he turned. 'Oh, by the way, sir, my Sergeant Malley—an awfully nice chap, you'll like him—asked me to remind you about the inquest. Do you think you could find time to pop in and have a word with him?'

'I suppose so. When?'

'It's stupid of me not to have mentioned it earlier, but I believe he hoped you would call this morning. Look, if you've nothing urgent on hand you can come over with me now.'

Lintz shrugged and reached down his hat and coat.

As he followed the inspector down the narrow, uncarpeted stairs, he asked: 'Who's this Sergeant Malley, anyway?'

'He's the Coroner's Officer,' replied Purbright, 'and the best baritone in the country, they tell me. You don't happen to be a singer, do you, sir?'

'No,' said Lintz, 'I don't.'

CHAPTER TWO

Lintz found Sergeant Malley awaiting him in the dark, file-cluttered little office that served as a clearing house for Flaxborough's uncertificated deaths.

The Coroner's Officer was florid, fat, catarrhal and kindly. He greeted the editor rather in the manner of a butcher anxious to placate a good customer for whom he had forgotten to reserve some kidneys.

'A bit of a nuisance, but there it is,' he said comfortingly as he turned a sheet of fresh paper into the typewriter before him. 'Now, sir, this is what the Coroner will have to refer to when you give your evidence tomorrow. What he'll do is just to ask the questions to guide you into saying the same as you're going to say now. Compree?"

Lintz replied somewhat coolly that he knew the procedure at inquests and was ready to help the sergeant prepare his disposition.

Malley began to type the formal introduction to the statement, muttering as he jabbed the keys and backspacing now and then to correct an error with vicious superimposition. The machine seemed to have the durability of a pile-driver.

'First he'll want you to say when you last saw your uncle alive. When will that have been, sir?'

'About six o'clock yesterday evening. I drove him back from the office in my car and left him at his home soon afterwards.'

Malley attacked the typewriter again. 'I drove ... deceased ...'

Lintz gazed round the tiny office and nibbled, quite fastidiously, the corner of a finger nail.

'And how did Mr Gwill strike you then, sir? In what sort of health, would you say?'

'The same as usual. I didn't notice anything wrong with him.'

Malley thought about this and fed his own version into the machine. '. . . usual good health . . .' he murmured. Then: 'I suppose he'd never given you cause to expect he might do anything a bit rash?'

'That he might commit suicide, you mean?'

'Well, you could put it that way. Had he been depressed? Worried?'

'If he had, he didn't confide in me.'

'Perhaps not, sir. But you could have formed an opinion of your own about his general mood.'

Malley, Lintz realized, was neither as simple as he looked nor likely to leave questions half answered for the sake of peace. 'My uncle was never particularly cheerful,' he conceded. 'He was an easily irritated man.'

'And had he been more touchy in recent weeks, or months?'

'For the last half year or so, yes, I think he had.'

'But you know of no special reason for that?'

'None. I didn't share his life at all outside the office and things have run perfectly smoothly there.'

'No bereavements of any kind, sir? Relatives? Friends?'

Lintz shook his head.

'Neighbours?' the sergeant persisted.

Lintz frowned, then gave one of his lop-sided smiles. 'Certainly a neighbour of his died a few months ago. It would be remarkable if one hadn't. They're nearly all over seventy round there.'

'Mr Carobleat wasn't very old, sir?'

'I really couldn't say.'

'Were they friendly, he and your uncle?'

'They were next-door neighbours.'

'Nothing beyond that?'

'I don't know.' Lintz knew the effectiveness of an unqualified negative.

'What it all amounts to, then, is that Mr Gwill appeared rather moodier than usual over the past six months but that he didn't tell you what was on his mind. Can I put it like that, sir?'

'For what it's worth, yes.'

Malley nodded and began to type again. At the end of a few more lines he read back to himself all he had put down so far. He looked up at Lintz. 'I'm not sure there's much more you can say that would help.'

'That's what I was thinking.'

'Of course, there's the identification. We might as well add that now.' The onslaught on the typewriter was resumed. '. . . a body . . . been shown . . . now identify . . .'

Lintz felt he might be permitted a question for a change. 'What sort of a verdict is possible in a case like this?'

Malley shrugged. 'I can't say what view the Coroner will take, of course, sir,' he replied guardedly. 'He'll sit without a jury, otherwise heaven knows what the verdict would be. Last week, a bunch wanted to return "found drowned" on a bloke who propped himself up against the harbour wall with half a pint of disinfectant inside him.'

'And the Coroner?'

'Oh, Mr Amblesby, you know, sir. Quite a character.' Malley left Lintz to interpret that for himself.

'The inspector came round to see me this morning. That's a little unusual, isn't it?'

'Bless you, no, sir.' Malley seemed amused. 'Mr Purbright's a conscientious gentleman. But you mustn't go thinking he's Scotland Yard or something. It's just that we have to look into these things, that's all.'

Lintz did not pursue the point. 'Anything more you want to ask me, sergeant?' He offered a cigarette.

'I don't think so, sir.' Malley accepted a light and pushed across the paper he had pulled from the typewriter. 'Read it over and see if you can think of anything we ought to add.'

Both men smoked in silence a while. Then Lintz drew out a fountain pen and signed the statement without further comment.

'Oh, there's one other thing while you're here, sir.' Malley was heaving himself from his chair. 'You'd better take these now and sign for them.'

He groped along a shelf high on the wall and reached down a canvas bag. Carefully he shook its contents on to the desk. 'We took these from his pockets,' he explained.

Lintz saw two or three envelopes, a little money, keys and a few other oddments. The sergeant gave the canvas a final shake. Unexpectedly, a paper bag hit the desk and burst, scattering several white, round objects soundlessly over its surface. Lintz picked one up, felt and sniffed it. 'Marshmallow,' he said, lamely.

'Oh, that's what they are.' Malley peered at the sweets and took an envelope from a drawer. 'I'd better put them in this.' He sat down and gathered the marshmallows into a pile.

When Lintz had pushed the filled envelope with the other things into his overcoat pocket he wrote his name quickly on the slip the sergeant had handed him and stood up.

'Half-past ten in the morning, sir,' said Malley. 'And don't worry. It'll all be very straightforward, I'm sure.'

*   *   *

Inspector Purbright stood at the entrance to The Aspens and looked with distaste at the large, naked house. Its brick face was a raw red, as if it blushed still for the intrusion into a secluded outskirt by its first owner, a successful bootlace manufacturer. Behind the tall, symmetrical windows, green curtains had been drawn. The semicircular lawn, lightly frosted now, its flanking gravel drive and the laurel-planted beds beyond, all looked sour and sullen. They wore the depressing neatness of ground laid out expressly to save the bother of gardening.

Purbright entered the drive past a high, wrought iron gate that had been swung back against the hedge and latched to a concrete stop. He walked up to the porched, dun-coloured front door and knocked. Almost immediately, he was looking into the red-rimmed, frightened eyes of a woman of about fifty, whose face hung in grey folds around an incongruously full-blooded and pert little mouth.

Mrs Poole led him through a lofty corridor to her own sitting room at the back of the house. It smelled of damp laundry and biscuits. Purbright accepted a seat and watched the late owner's housekeeper subside nervously into an armchair that looked more like a pile of old covers. She took the cigarette he offered, lit it with a paper spill and drew in the smoke like religion.

'An unpleasant experience for you, ma'am,' said the inspector.

'Shocking. Oh, shocking!' rustled the voice of Mrs Poole. She looked straight at him and twitched her sagging cheeks. 'I shouldn't have left him, you know.'

'You think not?'

'Oh, no. He should never have been on his own. I know that now. But I wasn't to be sure before. Mind you, he didn't ask me to stay. He'd never have done that. But now . . .' She went on staring at the mild, benign, yellow-haired man, apparently content that he had taken her meaning.

Purbright tried to do so. 'He wasn't too well; was that it?' he asked.

'He was well enough,' retorted Mrs Poole, 'but health never would have saved him. What was waiting for him didn't take account of whether he came running or wheeled in a chair.'

Purbright remembered Lintz's estimate of the housekeeper. 'Just you tell me what you think happened to him, then,' he invited.

The woman frowned and carefully tapped the ash from her cigarette into an empty tea cup by her chair.

'I don't know whether you believe in phenomenons,' she began, pausing to sharpen her regard of the inspector, 'but it doesn't matter if you do or don't. There are such things, though they take a bit of understanding. Some spiritualists—and I don't call myself that, mind—some say there's nothing but good in what comes to us in that way. But never you believe them. It stands to sense that if the living's good and bad mixed, then those who've passed over are two sorts as well. Only even more so, if you see what I mean.'

She left off to poke the small, smouldering fire, but seemed to expect no comment. 'What we call possession,' she resumed, 'is just the bad kind getting hold of someone here to be spiteful with. That's all in books, so there's no call for Mr Clever-pants Lintz to be so certain of himself. Not that he ever worried about his uncle's troubles. There's none so blind as those who won't see. Mr Lintz never even noticed when it started in the summer. His uncle wasn't as scared then as he got afterwards, of course, but I could have told you to the day when he first knew— Mr Gwill, I mean.'

Purbright found the flow of urgent, husky speech fascinating in spite of his sense of time being wasted on a woman half frightened, half hypnotized by her own fancies. He listened in silence, gazing first at one piece of furniture, then another, but avoiding now the eyes which had brightened with the fever-fire of psychic exposition.

'It all started a month to the day after that one'—she jabbed with her cigarette towards the wall beside her—'was put in his grave. He'd always been a quiet sort, had Mr Gwill, but dignified, you know. He didn't show his feelings as a rule. But four weeks after the funeral from next door, I saw him trembling and clenching in the big room as if he'd got pneumonia. "Excuse me, sir," I said, "but are you feeling all right?" He looked at me as if he'd never seen me before and shot straight out of the house. And he was never the same after that. Sometimes he was better, sometimes worse, but he couldn't really settle.'

'I thought this man, Mr Carobleat, was a friend of his,' Purbright observed.

'A friend, sir?' Mrs Poole's chubby mouth twisted in derision. 'Him?'

'That's only what I've been told.'

'Oh, they were thick enough at one time. That Mr Carobleat was always in and out. But he wasn't Mr Gwill's kind. I couldn't stand him, he was that sly and for ever m'dear-ing me as if I was a barmaid or something. And he hung about so . . .'

Purbright looked back from contemplation of the dresser to catch Mrs Poole staring at the window behind him. 'Yes,' he prompted, 'go on.'

Mrs Poole straightened. She shook her head doubtfully. 'I don't think I should say any more, sir.'

Purbright waited but she remained silent.

At last he said, 'You weren't in the house last night, I understand.'

'No, sir. I'd gone over to my sister's. I got the eight o'clock train back this morning.'

'Yes, I'm only sorry you could have had no warning. It must have been a shock.'

'Oh, the policeman here was very kind. He told me what . . . what had happened.' Mrs Poole delved into the bundle-like chair and drew out a small handkerchief, with which she nervously dabbed the end of her nose.

'Do you happen to know if Mr Gwill was worried about business affairs?'

Mrs Poole looked blank. 'You'd have to ask Mr Lintz about that, sir.'

'He didn't appear to think there was anything wrong.'

'Then there can't have been, I suppose. Mr Gwill wouldn't have said anything to me, in any case.'

'But he was upset about something?'

Again the woman's eyes flickered towards the window. In a suddenly decisive tone she declared: 'He was being pestered, sir, and that's the top and bottom of it.'

The inspector leaned forward slightly. 'By whom?'

'No one you could lay *your* hands on, sir.'

Back to where we started, Purbright told himself. 'Would you say . . .' he said slowly, '. . . would you say that Mr Gwill knew precisely what he was doing when the accident happened?'

'Ac-cident?' The scornfully stressed first syllable expressed Mrs Poole's opinion of people who supposed her late employer might have ever done anything save with reason and intention.

'You think,' suggested Purbright, 'that he could have done what he did deliberately?'

Mrs Poole ground out her cigarette stub—it was surprisingly short, the inspector noticed—against the fire back, and flicked her fingers over her pinafore. 'Not that, either,' she said. 'He was trying to get away, that's all. Poor soul,' she added, almost to herself.

Back again.

'Tell me, Mrs Poole, did Mr Gwill have any regular visitors?'

'Well, only the people you'd expect. Mr Lintz came sometimes, of course. He'd never stay for long, though. Not for meals. Then Mr Gloss came over occasionally, and . . .'

'Mr Gloss?'

'Yes, sir. The solicitor. He'd sometimes bring Dr Hillyard with him, but just as often the doctor came on his own.'

'Mr Gwill wasn't having treatment, though?'

'Oh, no—at least, not as far as I know. The doctor came in the evenings. He'd usually stay for dinner. There were times when I served for him and Mr Gwill and Mr Gloss and Mr Bradlaw as well. The . . . the builder.'

Purbright noticed her reluctance to name Mr Bradlaw's main occupation. 'Those three gentlemen were personal friends of Mr Gwill, I take it.'

'They were, sir.'

'And no one else called here regularly?'

Mrs Poole did not reply for a few moments. Then she nodded towards the wall beyond which she had previously indicated 'that one', and said coldly: 'Only her.'

'Mrs Carobleat?'

'Now and again. Once a week, maybe.'

'Another personal friend?' Purbright avoided putting the slightest emphasis on any of the three words.

'Not of mine,' Mrs Poole hastily asserted, 'and more than that I can't say.'

Purbright stood up. 'I wonder,' he said gently, 'if you'd mind very much my taking a quick look round

the house? You don't have to say yes if you'd rather
Mr Lintz were here to give permission.'

Mrs Poole sniffed. 'I'm not employed by Mr Lintz,
sir, and I'm sure his permission doesn't matter much
in this house.'

'You are agreeable, then?'

'You're the police, sir. You're welcome to see what
you've a mind to.'

She carefully placed four lumps of coal on the fire
and rose. 'Which rooms were you wanting to look at?'

'Where did he do most of his work, Mrs Poole? Assuming that he did work at home.'

The housekeeper led the way along the corridor
and opened a door. 'This was where he spent quite a
lot of his time.'

Purbright entered a small room that contained an
elderly roll-top desk, a big table faced with leather,
and two office chairs. Brown velvet curtains hung at
the single window. Over the desk was a bare light
bulb, its flex anchored to the picture rail by a length
of twine. The room looked like the office of a not
very successful suburban lawyer or a part-time regis-
trar.

Purbright padded round the table and glanced into
a wall cupboard. It was empty except for a thick file
of newspapers. Near the window, he bent down and
picked from the floor a piece of silky material, a
headsquare or small scarf. He handed it to Mrs Poole.

She shook it out with faint distaste. 'Something of
hers, I suppose,' she said, folding it quickly and putting it on a dusty, black-painted mantelpiece beside a
stone ink bottle and a spike of faded cuttings.

'Not what you might call a cosy room,' Purbright
remarked.

'Mr Gwill didn't like to use anywhere else when he
had business to attend to. He used to say no one
could work properly if they were comfortable.'

'Then it seems Mrs Carobleat called partly, if not altogether, for business reasons?'

Mrs Poole stared at him, then glanced at the folded scarf. 'I don't know why she came. She used to push her own way around and I always kept clear until I heard her leave.'

Purbright gave the desk cover a casual trial with one finger. It was unlocked and slid back easily. The compartments inside contained a few tidily stacked papers. He did not disturb them. Instead, he flicked through several of the books that lay there. The first two were ledgers. The third contained newspaper clippings. They had been taken from classified advertisements columns and pasted into the book, a couple of dozen or so to each page.

The inspector read quickly through a few of them. 'Was Mr Gwill interested in buying and selling furniture, d'you know?' he asked.

Mrs Poole shook her head. 'Not specially. He bought a sideboard about a year ago. A bit before that we had the dining-room chairs re-seated.' She looked doubtfully at the book. 'That's all office stuff. He kept some of it here and worked on it in the evenings sometimes.'

Purbright showed her the open pages. 'You wouldn't know why he kept these, I suppose?'

She peered at the cuttings. 'They're adverts,' she said unhelpfully, 'from the paper.'

'Oh,' said Purbright. He closed the book, put it back with the others and drew down the desk top.

Mrs Poole stood aside as he left the room. She closed the door behind them and asked if he wished to see anything else. Purbright hesitated. 'There's the bedroom,' prompted Mrs Poole.

'I'm a terrible old nuisance, aren't I?' he said brightly, as they moved towards the staircase.

'That's all right, sir. I only want it all to be settled and no more harm done to anyone.' She reached the landing and turned off towards a second, shorter flight.

Purbright silently kept pace with the housekeeper along a passage that he judged to correspond with the corridor below.

She stopped before a door almost at the end. They were at the back of the house. The air was cold and damp.

Mrs Poole looked at him earnestly. 'Do you know when they'll be bringing him home?' she asked. 'I thought I'd better keep this room ready.'

'I'm afraid I can't tell you definitely, but it shouldn't be later than tomorrow. You understand that what we call a post-mortem examination has had to be made?'

'I see.' She opened the door quietly and motioned him in. The room was dim but the outlines of its few pieces of furniture showed it to be spacious and arranged with austere practicality. Purbright walked slowly across to the window, pulled the curtain slightly aside, and looked out.

Below was the large back garden, dank and shrubby. A line of poplars screened its end like huge brooms stuck handles down in the earth. Weak winter sunshine fell aslant one of the two flanking walls. The bushes were motionless and dark against the frost-whitened soil.

Purbright let the curtain fall and re-crossed the room. The woman said nothing. He went past her and waited for her to close the door. Her eyes, he saw, had become slow and devoid of expression, like raisins in the dough of her face.

He put his hand on her arm. 'What has been frightening you, Mrs Poole?'

She looked up and caught her breath. Then she gave a jerky little smile and replied: 'Nothing frightens me, sir. Not now. I think it's over.'

She began to lead the way back along the passage.

CHAPTER THREE

Inspector Purbright did not pay his promised call on the lonely widow of Mr Carobleat. As he walked out through the open gate of The Aspens, he noticed activity in the field beyond the fence on the opposite side of the road and crossed over.

Detective Sergeant Sidney Love was gloomily trudging around in the grass, followed closely by a confused-looking uniformed constable. As Purbright joined them, he saw a small wooden stake driven into the ground a few feet from the base of the power supply mast.

Love eyed him without enthusiasm. 'We've taken measurements, sir.'

Purbright gazed up at the pylon. 'What an odd perch for a newspaper proprietor,' he murmured. 'Power without responsibility, I suppose.'

'Is there anything else we can do?' Love asked. 'It's jolly cold here.'

'Have you measured the height of the cable arm?'

'What, climbed up, do you mean, sir?' The sergeant looked incredulously at the steel network.

'Maybe it's pointless,' Purbright conceded. 'Call it twenty-five feet, shall we? No, twenty-seven—that'll sound as if we really know.' He walked slowly round the stake, scuffing the grass here and there with his shoe. 'Nothing round here, Sid?'

'What had you in mind, sir?'

Purbright looked at Love from under his brows. 'Clues,' he said. 'Cloth fibres. Nail parings. Dust from a hunch-backed grocer's shop. You know.'

'Wilkinson here found a mushroom.'

'In December?'

'It wasn't up to much. I advised him to throw it away.'

'In that case we might as well get back into town. I've already spent a useless half hour in that mausoleum over there. Mrs what's-her-name should flee to relatives before she works herself into a state of demoniac possession.'

Love glanced at him. 'She gave you that sort of tale, did she?'

'She did indeed. It was rather like the "Cat and the Canary". Come on; you're right, it is cold.'

'Mrs Poole isn't the only one with queer ideas about this business.' Love kicked the stake from side to side, drew it out and handed it to the constable. 'There's talk at some of the farms about hauntings and what have you. That's right, isn't it, Wilk?'

Wilkinson frowned as he waited for the others to climb over the fence. 'Mind you, sir,' he said to Purbright, 'it wouldn't do to believe everything they say down this end. They think telling lies is a great joke down here—more especially if it's likely to give us fellows a job to do for nothing.'

'Yes, but you told me you'd heard this latest tale direct from a cousin or something,' Love put in.

'That's right, sir.'

'Go on then, man,' urged the sergeant.

Wilkinson looked a little resentful. He had not intended a piece of country gossip, passed on in an effort to cheer a chilled and chilly C.I.D. man, to be officially reported to the bland and (he had heard) 'sarky' inspector. But Purbright, walking now almost paternally between them, turned upon the constable a look of kindly encouragement.

'Well, sir,' said Wilkinson, 'I've no reason to believe this nor to expect you to, but according to this relative of mine—he has a garage a bit along the road there—some of the country people have had the notion for a while now that some sort of a ghost was trying to get into Mr Gwill's house. It sounds daft, put like that'—the constable reddened—'and I wouldn't think of repeating such nonsense except for something this chap says he saw himself latish on last night. He was cycling home from town when he saw Mr Gwill just behind that gate of his and splashing water about on the ground from a big jar or a can. It was pretty dark, but Maurice was sure about the water. He could hear it slosh as he went by.'

Purbright had listened carefully; now he asked: 'And what did your cousin think was significant about that?'

The constable flushed more deeply still. 'The tale goes that it was holy water in that pot. . . . But it doesn't seem to make much sense. I only mentioned it, like, to the sergeant here . . .' He broke off.

'Jolly interesting little story, anyway,' said Purbright, rescuing Wilkinson from his embarrassment. 'It helps to give us a picture of the fellow, which is more than I can get from the people who are supposed to have known him. You were quite right to tell us, constable.'

The trio made its way through the streets of the town without further conversation. Purbright liked staring about him when he was out and silently guessing the errands of such inhabitants as were not leaning against something. Love watched presentable young females from behind his disguise of pink-faced singlemindedness. As for Wilkinson, he ruminated on the inspector's lack of 'side' and thought up ways of proclaiming it, with some small credit to himself, in the parade room later on.

One of the first things Purbright saw when he entered the police station was the unmistakable rear of Sergeant Malley, who was leaning over the reception counter to talk to the duty officer. In the centre of the serge acreage of his trousers seat was a round, white blemish. Purbright stopped and tapped his shoulder. 'You seem to have sat on something,' he confided.

Malley's hand stole searchingly down. Having peeled off what he could of the white substance, he stared at his fingers. 'It's one of those bloody marshmallows,' he announced.

'What bloody marshmallows?'

'The one's from old Gwill's pocket. It must have fallen on my chair when I was collecting his stuff together for Lintz to take away.'

'Oh,' said Purbright. He walked off to his own office.

Sergeant Love joined him. As there were now no girls to be regarded, he had allowed his face to resume its expression of slightly petulent innocence. Purbright looked upon it thoughtfully; he could never quite decide whether that cleanly shining feature properly belonged to a cherub or an idiot.

'Please forgive me'—the inspector had lifted the telephone—'the pathology block at the General. Doctor Heineman.' He leaned back against his desk and waited.

A mittel-European voice chimed brightly over the wire. "Mornink, inspector!'

'Good morning, doctor. Finished with that gentleman we asked you to look at?'

'But yes. You are requirink him back again?'

'What killed him?'

'Failure of heart, naturally. But before that there was asphyxia and before that shock from the electrics and nothing before that except joys and sorrows and delusions, dear chappie. A report I'm sendink you any minute. You must think I've somethink worse to do. I don't play golf all day, you guess. How's that funny little fellow that scrubs the face with carbolic or what? When's he come and see us cuttink-up merchants again; that's how he calls us, I know that. No, but I'm so busy now. Got what you wanted?'

'Stomach contents?'

'Ha, all sorts. Very jolly. Why?'

'Anything unusual?'

'Nothink corrodink, I should say. Want them done?'

'Not if you're happy about the cause of death.'

'He was not poisoned. That I tell you. Shock and everythink; that was it.'

'Very well, doctor. Oh, by the way . . .'

'Yes?'

'Did you notice anything about the mouth? Any trace of recent food?'

'But yes, yes . . . both teeth pieces, top and bottom, they are sticky—gummy, how is it? He would be eatink sweets, that fellow.'

'Soft, white sweets?'

'Exactly so.'

'Thank you, doctor. You'll let me have the full report as soon as you can. The inquest will be adjourned, by the look of things; you needn't bother to turn up tomorrow unless you hear.'

As Purbright put down the telephone, Love gave him a questioning look. 'Why the morbid interest in diet?'

'Because,' said Purbright, 'I have yet to find a man of Gwill's age who can clamber up towers in the middle of the night with his mouth full of marshmallows. Because I have never encountered a suicide who has been in the mood for confectionery at the last moment. And because I cannot believe that any newspaper owner would be anxious, even in sudden insanity, to court the kind of publicity he has caused to be inflicted on others.'

'You don't think he was electrocuted, then?'

'Oh, yes, he was. Heineman may imagine you wash your face in carbolic, but he doesn't make mistakes with corpses. Anyway, there were signs of burning, I believe; we'll know for sure when the P.M. report comes in.' He paused. 'Have you ever had anything to do with the nephew?'

'George Lintz? I've run across him occasionally.'

'A close gentleman.'

Love shrugged. 'Careful, certainly. Do you think he knows anything?'

'Hard to say. You might have a go at him. He resists the suave approach. Try your bike-without-lights manner.'

'What times do you want him to account for?'

'Last night from sixish until whatever time he says he went to bed. He is married, isn't he?'

'That's right.'

'In that case, try her as well. See if she has the Lady Macbeth touch. Cocktail cabinet catalogues on the kitchen table: that sort of thing. Before you go, you might take a look at his statement to Malley. There are one or two other things I'd better tell you, although they amount to very little so far.' He described the interview with Lintz and his visit to The Aspens.

'Don't you think there might be something behind the ghoulies and ghosties business?' Love suggested.

'I wouldn't write it off,' Purbright replied. 'Mrs Poole obviously believes in "the withering touch of tomb-escaped avenger". She's been frightened, undoubtedly, but she'll not say by what or whom.'

'She may be a bit touched, of course.'

'Yes, but there are other tales than hers, apparently.'

Love pouted. 'Will you get an adjournment tomorrow?'

'Oh, certainly. Not for long, though. Gwill was a fairly important fellow. There'll be some pressure to have him put under without any unseemly inquiries. We shall have to produce a convincing argument within the next week or so.'

'There's the point about the marshmallow, or whatever it was.'

Purbright waved his hand contemptuously. 'I can just hear old Albert on that. . . . "Eatin' sweets, was he, eh? And why not, eh? Better than drinkin' himself silly." '

The inspector's opinion of Mr Albert Amblesby was well founded. Flaxborough's coroner was an ancient of such obtuseness that the inquiries over which he presided were liable to deteriorate into ill-tempered games, with Mr Amblesby inventing new rules and breaking old ones, deriding what he couldn't understand and generally playing hell until he could glare around his court and judge from the silence of the other angry, unhappy or bewildered contestants that he had won.

'You'd better ask Malley to come in. He might know something that will give us a lead.'

Love returned with the outsize Coroner's Officer, breathing hard.

Sergeant Malley seemed pleased rather than surprised by Purbright's suspicion. 'Murder,' he observed, 'wouldn't half be a nice change.'

'What do you know about Gwill's affairs?' Purbright asked him.

'Not a deal. He kept very much to himself. Rather a gloomy chap, I always thought. He was supposed to be carrying on with that Carobleat woman, you know.

Not that that would have set anyone on fire, I expect. Anyway, not once her old man had upped and died. He had plenty of money, of course—Gwill, I mean. Or so they say.'

'But he didn't collect jealous husbands?'

'Not as you'd notice.'

'Did he have any other kind of enemies, do you know?'

Malley pursed his lips. 'Well . . . put it this way. Nobody liked him. Does that help?'

'Enormously,' said Purbright. 'I do like a big field.'

Love spoke. 'But he had a circle of friends, surely?'

'Oh, yes,' said Malley. 'Circle is the word.'

'Exclusive?'

'Like the reptile house.'

'Come now,' protested Purbright, 'we must try to be objective about this. The list the wild-eyed house-keeper gave me was respectable enough. Wait a minute. . . .' He took an envelope from his pocket. 'Yes, there's a doctor for a start. Hillyard—you know him?'

'Dipsomaniac,' retorted the unrepentant Malley.

'Medical Officer of Health-elect,' said Purbright, comfortingly. 'Then there's Bradlaw the burier. Blameless, surely. We've nothing on Nab Bradlaw, have we?'

Love shook his head. Malley grunted.

Again Purbright glanced at the list. 'Rodney Gloss, man of law.'

'Straight as an acrobat's intestines.' This from the stout sergeant.

Purbright sighed. 'I think,' he said, 'that we can start from the sound assumption that people seldom get themselves murdered by complete strangers. At the same time, we shall need to begin inquiring into what, if any, were Gwill's departures from the normal and legitimate. Also, I propose to have a word with

the Chief Constable and try and persuade him—God
give me strength—that there is good reason to suspect
that Gwill was done.

'And we needn't hope to be spared trouble by old
Chubb deciding to "call in the Yard", as I believe the
phrase goes. For one thing, he likes to keep misfor-
tune in the family. For another, he'd probably be hes-
itant to bother such a busy man as Sir Robert Peel.'

CHAPTER FOUR

While Purbright was fortifying himself with food against the approaching ordeal by Chief Constable, Mr Harcourt Chubb, himself—a slow thinker and late eater—listened to a lawyer's tale.

It was Mr Rodney Gloss who had called upon him.

The Chief Constable, silver-haired, composed and misleadingly aesthetic-looking, regarded his visitor with polite attention and a perpetual half-smile.

Gloss had put himself at a disadvantage by accepting a seat before he remembered that the Chief Constable habitually remained standing, even in his own drawing room. He was, therefore, obliged to crane a bull-like neck in order to keep Chubb in the focus of his little fierce eyes.

The solicitor spoke quietly and carefully.

'I need scarcely point out,' he began, 'that what I am about to say is in the strictest confidence. It may be impossible of confirmation. I certainly wish, at this stage, to accept no personal part in the matter and to bear no responsibility for the veracity of anything I now mention.'

Mr Chubb nodded graciously. The solicitor turned further round in his chair and rested his folded arms along the back of it.

'You may be aware that I am—or was, rather—an acquaintance of Marcus Gwill, of whose shocking death I was apprised a short while ago. Indeed, he

was my client. Naturally, I am aware of the details of
how he is supposed to have died, but I have heard
the rumours that follow upon an incident of this
kind. You will perhaps tell me if I am correct in be-
lieving the circumstances to have pointed to electrocution.'

Again Mr Chubb nodded.

'I see,' said Gloss. 'My further information is that
there were no witnesses of this unfortunate occur-
rence and that its nature is surmised on the strength
of Marcus having been found beneath the electricity
pylon opposite his house.'

'The police have no reason to suspect anything but
an accident, if that is what you mean,' observed the
Chief Constable. 'A peculiar accident, certainly, but
one that is not inconceivable.'

'Were I to say my conviction—my purely instinctive
conviction, if you like—is that Gwill's death was not
accidental, would you be prepared to be guided by
that without my providing evidence to support it?'

Chubb raised an eyebrow. 'Might you explain what
you have in mind, Mr Gloss?'

'That is just the point, my dear sir. The situation is
such that I can give precious little explanation. I am,
in a sense, a materialization of an anonymous letter
writer. The anonymous letter, as we both know well,
is given no less consideration by the police than a
signed one, providing its contents promise to be useful. I could have gone to the rather absurd and distasteful length of pasting clipped-out words to a sheet
of paper and sending you that, but I prefer to act
straightforwardly and logically. In so doing, however,
I think I am entitled to claim immunity from in-
volvement.'

'Your duty, Mr Gloss, is to help the police in whatever way you can, especially if you have reason to suspect a crime has been committed.'

'I am a solicitor, Mr Chubb, and well aware of what citizens are supposed to do. I am also aware of how seldom they do what they should, and of how little the police can do to make them. That is why I am here now instead of concocting a mysterious message from newspaper clippings. You and I are civilized, sophisticated and, let us admit it, privileged persons, who can afford to be advised by each other without going through all the wasteful, compromising nonsense of "official procedure".'

Chubb paced slowly across the carpet and back. Standing before the fire, he regarded his fingernails thoughtfully. 'I think you're quite wrong, you know,' he said.

'In what respect?'

'In supposing Gwill to have been murdered. That is what you mean to imply, isn't it?'

'It is.' Gloss looked at him steadily.

'But that's absurd. The man wasn't robbed. No one stuck a knife into him. He hadn't run off with someone's wife; I'd have heard soon enough at the club if he had. No, it's not nice to say of a chap who always seemed absolutely sensible and level-headed, but it's perfectly obvious that he must have gone off his chump all of a sudden in the night. You and I can see that, but there'll be no need for the town to make a song and dance of it. The local paper can hardly do anything else but soft pedal. You know he owned it, I suppose?'

'Of course. I was his solicitor and I presume I shall continue to handle the legal affairs of the company. But we are straying a little from the point. The very fact that I stood in a professional relationship to Gwill surely should carry weight when I tell you that he was not without enemies.'

'Few of us are, Mr Gloss.'

'I might also add . . .' Gloss hesitated.

'Yes?'

'It should be understood, perhaps, that my motives for approaching you on this matter are not entirely altruistic. You see, I am not confident that my own safety is henceforth assured.'

Chubb blinked. 'What do you mean?'

'Simply that I am extremely apprehensive. For what other reason do you suppose I might have come to see you? To put it absolutely baldly, I am asking you to provide—unobtrusively and unofficially—what I suppose we must call police protection.'

'But protection against what, man?' The slightest suggestion of fluster had crept into the Chief Constable's voice.

'I cannot tell you. You will just have to trust me when I say that I have ample cause to be alarmed and to urge you to regard the death of Marcus Gwill as deliberately contrived—and perhaps the prelude to further crimes. Believe me, Mr Chubb, I have no desire to seem guilty of sensationalism, but when the alternative is to await in silence another curious accident of which I may be the victim, I am prepared to shed a little dignity.'

The precise phraseology was maintained, but upon the solicitor's brow and neck had appeared a gleaming dew.

Chubb, too, looked uncomfortable. He shook his head. 'I'm afraid any special arrangements by us would be out of the question. We haven't the men available, and even if we had I couldn't authorize the individual protection of someone who won't say what he wants to be protected against.'

Gloss compressed his lips and stared at the thin, rather loose figure of the Chief Constable leaning lightly against the fireplace. He decided to make one more attempt.

'Naturally,' he said, 'I do not ask for the attendance of a . . . a bodyguard, in what I conceive to be the American sense. The contingency I envisage is not likely to arise during daylight. Would it be out of the question to augment your normal night patrol in the St Anne's Place area with an officer charged simply with keeping my house under observation?'

Chubb sighed. 'Why don't you tell me what this is all about? Surely you see how difficult you make it for me to help. Let us be frank, Mr Gloss. Who is threatening you?'

'Please believe me when I say it is no one against whom you could possibly take action.'

'Yet you imply that whoever it is has already committed murder.'

'All I wish you to realize is that someone of homicidal intentions is at large, someone clever enough to have misled your men on one occasion and capable of doing so again.'

Chubb put his hand in his pocket and jingled change. Patiently, he asked: 'How, do you suggest, was Gwill killed?'

'I have no idea. That, surely, is for your officers to discover from the evidence. The crime must have been carefully and perhaps elaborately planned.'

'And with what motive was he killed?'

'In revenge, perhaps . . . or to gratify sheer evil-mindedness. But again, we digress. May I have your answer to the question I put a few moments ago?'

'I have already given it, Mr Gloss. I'm sorry.'

Whatever the solicitor felt, he showed nothing. Briskly he rose and brushed his stiff black hat with the sleeve of his overcoat.

At the front door, the Chief Constable gave parting advice. It was a brief homily about the inadvisability of withholding information from the police. He had no confidence that it would do any good. And, indeed, it didn't.

* * *

Some twenty minutes later, Chubb's enjoyment of a delayed lunch was modified by his wife's announcement that Inspector Purbright had called and was awaiting him in the front room. He immediately concluded that the damnable affair of the electrocuted newspaper proprietor had taken a turn for the worse and that Purbright bore confirmation of the forebodings of his earlier visitor. He champed his apple tart mournfully and wandered, still nibbling a clove, into the drawing-room.

He found the inspector examining the plaster statuette of a yellow-haired Venus, petrified into Art while apparently picking a corn.

'I suppose,' said Chubb without preamble, 'that you've come about Gwill.'

Purbright nodded. 'I'm afraid I have, sir,' he said, as though breaking the news of the running over of one of Chubb's Yorkshire terriers—in other words, with just enough pretence of regret to hide a real inward satisfaction.

The Chief Constable motioned him to a chair and took up his own position of command and disparagement by the fireplace. 'Carry on, my boy,' he said.

Purbright carried on. He described the finding of the body that morning by a farm labourer on his way to work. Gwill had been wearing an overcoat, unbuttoned, over his suit, and a pair of slippers—sturdy leather ones, certainly, but slippers. He had lain, apparently since late the previous night, in the grass beneath the power pylon from which he was assumed at first to have fallen; at least, that theory had been adopted as soon as burns were seen on both his hands by the policeman who removed the body.

The front door of Gwill's house had been found closed but not latched. The drive gate was open. Gwill had been alone, probably, at the time he left his house, for the woman who looked after him had been staying elsewhere overnight.

Purbright gave the gist of what Lintz and Mrs Poole had said and wound up with something about marshmallows that sounded sinister and, thought the Chief Constable, a bit psychological as well, which was worse.

'Are you quite sure,' he asked when the inspector had done, 'that you aren't making too much of this?'

'Quite sure, sir,' said Purbright simply.

'Ah . . .' Chubb considered a moment. 'So we'd better take a closer look into things, then; that's what you think?'

'It does seem indicated.'

'Mmm . . .' Another pause. Then, 'It's rather odd,' said Chubb, 'and I'd better mention this while I remember, but you're the second chap to come along here today with doubts of this business having been quite above board.'

'Really, sir?'

'Yes. That solicitor with the thick neck and the bow tie—Humpty, I always call him—was here just before you called. Gloss. You know him?'

'I've met him in court.'

'Ah, well, he was being very mysterious, and frightened, too, I should say. He seemed quite convinced that poor old Gwill had been murdered. I thought he was just being morbid, but there you are.'

'That's interesting, sir. Did he say how he'd come to that conclusion?'

'He didn't. He was very cagey. He asked if I could put a man on his house at night. I turned that down, of course. He wouldn't give a reason, you see.'

'I'll have a word with him later on, sir. If he's really nervous, he'll probably be more forthcoming after a night or two of listening to creaking floorboards. In the meantime, there'll be other people to question.

I've no notion at the moment of where to bore into this case, as it were. The little sounding I've been able to do so far hasn't produced any helpful echoes. You follow me, sir.'

'Yes, oh certainly,' responded Chubb with haste. 'I mean old Gwill wasn't the sort of fellow you'd expect to get murdered. Except by an employee, perhaps. They tell me that newspaper of his is a bit of a sweat shop.'

'We'll look into that side of it, of course, sir. At first sight, though, one would think George Lintz had most to gain. I believe the control of the business will go to him. On the other hand, there's the rather curious relationship that seems to have existed between Gwill and the Carobleat woman. You remember the Carobleat affair, I suppose, sir?'

The Chief Constable frowned. 'It's a bit late in the day to drag that up again, isn't it? After all, you didn't manage to find much at the time.'

'I wasn't likely to, considering all the books had disappeared,' said Purbright drily. 'What with the firm having evaporated overnight, the owner dead and the widow paralysed with ignorance, it was hardly to be expected that we'd fasten anything on anyone.'

'Just as well, perhaps. It wouldn't have done the town much good, you know. Anyway, it's done with now. By the way, would you like me to have a word with Amblesby? You'll want the inquest holding over a while, I expect.'

'If you wouldn't mind, sir. He'll probably take the suggestion more kindly from one of his own—' Purbright nearly said 'generation' but substituted 'neighbours' on remembering that the desiccated solicitor lived amidst dust and despotism in a mansion on the other side of Chubb's road.

'Very well. I'll ask him to adjourn it *sine die* or

pending inquiries or something so that you can all get your heads down for a bit. Bad business. . . .' The Chief Constable shook his head and devoutly wished the world were a great dog show with policemen having nothing to do but guard the trophies and hold leads.

Purbright made his way back towards the police station. As he was walking past the railway station, he noticed a woman in tweeds and flower-pot hat among a small crowd emerging from its portico. He crossed over and greeted her. 'I nearly called in to see you this morning, Mrs Carobleat.'

Joan Carobleat, a matron competently parcelled and attractive in a mature, leathery way, raised overmade-up brows and returned Purbright's smile. 'It's just as well you didn't then, inspector, isn't it?'

'You've been away?'

'I've just got back from Shropshire, as a matter of fact. Did you want to see me particularly? Oh, it's not'—she frowned mockingly—'not that business about the shop again, surely?'

'Your husband's firm. No, not that.' Purbright glanced around. 'I hoped you might let me know when it would be convenient for me to have a word with you.'

'Urgent?'

'Moderately.'

'Look, then: I'm dying for a cup of tea after that appalling journey. Why not come into Harlow's here? It won't be too hectic at this time of day.'

They took refuge in one of the inglenooky seats and Mrs Carobleat gave her order to a girl exhausted with the effort of carrying countless roast-lamb-onces to relays of predatory female shoppers.

When the crockery had ceased to vibrate from its percussive assembly before them, Purbright looked at

his companion and said: 'I only hope this will be con-
strued as proper. I don't normally interrogate in
teashops.'

'You're surely not afraid of being unfrocked or dis-
barred or something,' said Mrs Carobleat, warily test-
ing the almost red-hot handle of a teapot that
contained, paradoxically, lukewarm tea.

'We coppers never quite reconcile ourselves to living in a perpetual draught of uncharitable thoughts.'

'That's what comes of being such a suspicious lot
yourselves.' She spooned sugar evenly into both cups
without asking if Purbright took it, added milk and
poured the tea. She took a packet of cigarettes from
the pocket of her suit, lit one, and pushed the packet
across the table. 'Now then, what are you after?' she
asked, as if Purbright were a small boy suspiciously
anxious to wash up.

'Where did you spend last night, Mrs Carobleat?'
The question was mildly put, yet it sounded incisive.

'Oho, something new, not the silly old shop
business again, after all.'

'That, as village constables are supposed to say, is
as maybe?'

She stirred her tea reflectively. 'May I ask why you
want to know?'

'You tell me first. Then I'll let you have a question.'

'All right, then. Where did I spend last night? Most
of it, I should say, at The Brink of Discovery.'

'I beg your pardon?'

'I'm sorry; it's a geographical joke, but perhaps you
don't know Shropshire. The Brink of Discovery is a
pub, a small hotel rather, on the far side of
Shrewsbury.'

'Rather remote from Flaxborough?'

'I think it's my turn, isn't it, inspector? The reason
for you asking, please.'

'Your next-door neighbour was murdered last night.' Purbright's expression remained pleasant but his eyes were intent.

Mrs Carobleat took the cigarette quickly from her lips. 'Not Marcus?'

'Mr Gwill, yes.'

She stared at him for a few seconds, then looked into her cup. 'But that's extraordinary. Are you sure?' She brought her gaze to him again, not, he thought, without an effort.

'If I weren't sure, I'd scarcely be chasing around asking questions.'

'No; of course. That was silly of me. But it came as rather a surprise.'

'I fancy Mr Gwill was surprised, too.'

'You mean somebody actually killed him? Deliberately, I mean?'

'Yes.'

'Well, it's dreadful, isn't it?'

He waited for her to say more, but she continued to stare at him, blankly now but with self-control.

'I was wondering,' said Purbright, 'if you might have anything helpful to tell me?'

She gravely tapped the ash from her cigarette. 'I really can't see what you think I might know about it.'

'When did you leave home, Mrs Carobleat?'

'Fairly early yesterday morning.'

'You went straight over to Shropshire?'

She nodded.

'Would you care to tell me why?'

'Heavens, I often go down there. I need a change occasionally from this bleak marsh of a place. The Westcountry used to be my home.'

'I see.'

'And since my husband died, there's been nothing to stop me going where and when I like.'

'Except the expense, perhaps.'

'He provided for me.'

'Yes,' said Purbright, 'I suppose he did.'

The waitress drifted near, eyed them with sad disapproval, and retired to lean against the further wall like a martyr turned down by fastidious lions. Outside, a clock struck three. A yellowish darkness had begun to press up against the misted windows.

'What purpose did you have in visiting Mr Gwill, Mrs Carobleat?'

She raised her brows. 'Why should you think I did? Oh'—she smiled—'you've been talking to old Prowler Poole.'

'Well?'

'I don't see it can have anything to do with what you say happened last night, but I did pop in occasionally to keep him company. I'm often at a loose end. I think he welcomed seeing a new face now and then after that death's head of a housekeeper.'

'The two of you don't happen to share an interest in furniture, by any chance?'

'Furniture?' She frowned, then laughed. 'Do you mean did we do carpentry together?'

Purbright grinned back. 'Never mind.'

He was framing his next question when he saw Mrs Carobleat's face grow suddenly hard and alert. She watched the approach of someone whose footsteps Purbright could now hear behind him.

'Good afternoon to you.' A deep voice. Clipped Glaswegian accent and slightly sardonic tone.

Purbright half turned. Smiling down on him was an unusually tall man with splayed teeth and inflamed, protuberant eyes. His head was perched on the great promontory of his chest as though it had separate existence and might tumble off if it strained forward any further.

Mrs Carobleat spoke quietly. 'Inspector, this is Doctor Rupert Hillyard. Inspector Purbright. But you possibly know each other already.'

Dr Hillyard folded himself into a chair next to Purbright, who noticed the instinctive professionalism of his gesture of throwing, flap, flap, his gloves into his upturned hat, and then massaging the palm of one hand with the fingertips of the other. 'A shocking day, Inspector,' he observed portentously.

The doctor glared round the room over his shoulder, muttered 'Shocking' again, and transferred his attention back to Mrs Carobleat.

Hillyard's teeth fascinated Purbright. They were like bruised almonds that had been hastily stuck into his mouth at an angle and left to be supported on his lower lip. The effect was an impression of idiotic good nature that was not quite nullified by the calculation in the red-rimmed eyes. Sometimes he managed to hide his teeth; the effort produced a preposterous pout and high-hoisted eyebrows.

'You are being kept busy and out of mischief, lady, I trust?' he inquired of Mrs Carobleat.

'I am at present being tactfully helpful to the police,' she replied.

'Excellent. Though tact is not always what helps policemen, surely?' He turned inquiringly to Purbright. 'Discretion, however, can actually become obtrusive if pursued too far. Then it betrays. Is that not so, inspector?'

'I'm sure your patient would not take anything too far, doctor, not even discretion.'

'My patient?'

'I'm sorry. It was Mr Carobleat you attended, was it not?'

'Aye, that's so. God rest his soul.' This piety was delivered with a gentle shake of the head.

Mrs Carobleat eyed him coldly. 'It's God rest Marcus Gwill's soul as well, now, doctor.'

'As to that, lady, the sentiment does you credit. It does indeed.'

'I gather you were a friend of Mr Gwill,' Purbright put in. 'Is that so, doctor?'

'He was a patient of mine, inspector, and a very careful man.'

'He'd need to be.'

At this remark from Mrs Carobleat, Hillyard grinned and nudged Purbright. 'Ye hear tha' frae the wee body!' he chortled with grotesque bonhomie.

'For heaven's sake, drop that phoney Scottishry, Rupert.' Mrs Carobleat's voice had hardened, in spite of the familiarity.

Purbright looked at her for a moment, then rose from the table. 'I must be getting along,' he said. 'I'll come and see you at home some time, Mrs Carobleat, if I may.' He smiled at Hillyard. 'Goodbye for now, doctor.'

Hillyard, who had suddenly relapsed into mournful thoughtfulness, suspired a soft 'Aye'. Then he scowled and repeated the 'Aye' with dark, whiskilated ferocity.

CHAPTER FIVE

Seated in his own office again, Purbright was assailed by a sense not of the difficulty of his present task but of its remoteness from the orbit of his normal employment. The two were monstrously at odds. The routine whereby a small town was kept, as far as ordinary citizens could tell, a safe and well-ordered place had not been designed to cope with the ultimate in human desperation, any more than the Municipal Buildings had been designed to survive earthquakes. Purbright supposed that a murder could be solved by the same procedure as was used to detect a bicycle thief or the perpetrator of a charabanc outing swindle, and he was probably right. But what was missing was the comfort of precedent, the reassuring pattern of likelihood.

This crime was out of context. For one thing, its cleverness was uncharacteristic of Flaxborough, a town of earthy misdemeanours.

He did not even know how Gwill had been killed. His seeing through the arrangement of apparent accident or suicide had pleased him at first. But he now realized he had merely chopped down a tree to disclose a forest.

The post mortem report, now lying before him, confirmed Dr Heineman's earlier judgment. It added little of any significance. Yet there was one odd point.

Purbright glanced down the closely typed lines until he reached it again:

'Burns. The palms of both hands bore marks of recent superficial burning, suggestive of manual contact with a source of electric current. The left palm exhibited a transverse burn, three-quarters of an inch wide and three inches long. Ball of thumb on this side also slightly burned. On palm of right hand was a burn mark, star or flower shaped, clearly defined, approximately two and a half inches in diameter.'

Star or flower shaped. . . . Purbright knew little about electricity, but he was sure pylons bore no decorations of this kind. Where else were lethally charged stars or flowers to be found? He underlined the passage in the report and put it aside.

However Gwill had been killed, it could not have been done far from his own house. The slippers, the dumping of the body in the nearby field, the evidence of his having been seen late that night in the drive . . .

With a bucket of water, though: what explanation could there be for that piece of eccentricity?

Perhaps he had been as scared of ghosts as country neighbours—and Mrs Poole—supposed. She had said nothing specific, but there was no doubting the sort of fears she entertained. Yet that line of delusion was common enough. The police station complaint's book was crammed with the fancies of supersensitive menopause subjects, ears alert for sounds from the spirit world.

Another thing. Heineman had found no injury or mark on the body apart from the burns. Gwill had needed no forcible inducement to grasp his death. He must have suspected nothing. Had his murderer been a friend? A relation?

Gain . . . Lintz seemed the only candidate there, at least until all the ramifications of his uncle's financial position could be revealed. That might take time.

Gloss, as his solicitor, should be the best source of information.

But how helpful would he be? By the Chief's account, Gloss was touchy, odd, full of dark hints. Beneath his armour of professional canniness, he felt the sharp itch of fright. Police protection, indeed. Purbright could not remember such a request having been made in all his years with the Flaxborough force—not even when Alderman Hockley's perpetration of the first-night drugging of the Amateur Operatic Society cast of *Rose Marie* (four of the Mounties had actually marched comatosely into the orchestra pit) was unmasked.

Gloss had been Gwill's solicitor. But solicitors were not nowadays entertained to dinner by clients save in tokens of some more intimate relationship—or hold. Gwill seemed to have had an almost Edwardian penchant for entertaining professional men. The client of one guest. The patient of another. The potential subject (was that the word?) of a third.

The undertaker, Bradlaw.

A curious coterie, on the face of it. And yet there need have been nothing sinister in the association. Perhaps Gwill and his three friends (who had been four in Carobleat's day, the inspector reminded himself) had owed their affinity to nothing but a consciousness of being well-off by local standards.

Where did Mrs Carobleat come into things? The housekeeper obviously disliked her. But servants were notoriously sensitive to suggestions of immorality in their employers.

In turn, Mrs Carobleat seemed to have no love for Hillyard. Social jealousy? Or did she resent being the widow of a man whom Hillyard had failed to doctor successfully? Personal grievances against the medical faculty were not rare in Flaxborough. One's doctor was something one boasted about to friends, like a

cake recipe or a central heating system. It was hard to
have to admit a let-down.

Could Hillyard, Purbright wondered, have had a
hand in the snuffing of Gwill? It was conceivable that
Gwill had received, amongst the gossip that accompa-
nies the stream of news into a paper, knowledge of
some hideous professional blunder by Hillyard; that
he had threatened the doctor . . .

The thread of Purbright's speculation was broken
at this point by the entry of Sergeant Love.

Love unbuckled his raincoat and lit a cigarette. He
flicked through a few pages of his notebook, put it
back in his pocket and recited: 'I, Gladys Lintz, am a
married woman and forty-one years of age. I reside
with my husband, George, in a nice house and already have a cocktail cabinet, a free pass to the Od-
eon, two beautiful children and the Telly. What, kill
dear old Uncle Marcus? Why ever should I?'

'Quite,' said Purbright. 'Now tell me what she said
without really meaning to.'

'One, that husband George's cold feet woke her up
round about two o'clock this morning. Two, that she
had a vague idea that Uncle's affairs weren't all on
the up and up. Three, that she thinks the undertaker
did it. Four, that she takes that back on second
thoughts because Bradlaw's elder sister has had a lot
of trouble lately and she doesn't want to add to it.'

'You do invite confidences, don't you, Sid?'

'I'm every mother's bloody son,' replied Love, without rancour.

'But can we sort out anything useful?'

'Well, she made no secret of Lintz having been out
until the early hours. She thought he'd probably been
to the Cons Club.'

'We can ask him about that. In fact we'll have to,
now. Poor George is the best prospect we have at the
moment. But what was that she said about Gwill?'

Love took out his notes again. 'According to Gladys, her uncle had dealings with several people outside the newspaper business, and kept George in the dark about them. She doesn't know who they were and she's sure her husband was never able to find out. But the pair of them suspected the old man of making money on the side.'

'What sort of dealings? Buying and selling?'

'She hadn't a clue.'

Purbright considered a while. 'Look,' he said, 'I think we'll pull in a little of Gwill's homework. There's a cuttings book over at his house that keeps popping into my head for some reason or other. I'd like to see what you make of it.'

'Do you want us to go over there now?'

'Have something to eat first. Oh, and tell me about Mrs Lintz and Nab Bradlaw.'

'She said Gwill knew Bradlaw pretty well. . . .'

'So I've heard.'

'. . . and had said on one occasion something about "fixing him if he'd a mind to". She thought it sounded like a threat and suggested Bradlaw had done the fixing first.'

'Did she say when this threat was made?'

'Several months ago, apparently. At one time every undertaker used to get a free mention in the paper's report of any funeral he'd handled. Then the system was dropped. Nab was the only one to make a fuss and Lintz asked his uncle what he should do. Gwill told him to let Bradlaw go to hell and dropped that hint that Nab was in no position to be awkward.'

'Hardly an incident pregnant with murderous possibilities.'

'Not on the face of it. But Gwill wasn't in the habit of saying much, least of all in Gladys's hearing. The remark stuck in her mind. It's a very narrow mind,' Love explained.

*   *   *

An hour later, the inspector and the sergeant drove to The Aspens. Mrs Poole, compliant, but looking more than ever like an evicted cemetery-sitter, showed them straight to the room with the desk. Purbright explained to her that they were going to take away some books, but that everything would be reported to Mr Lintz and that she need not worry. She refuted the suggestion that anything Mr Lintz might think could worry *her* and gave them to understand that they would be welcome to take away Mr Lintz as well.

'No one,' observed Purbright as he accompanied a book-laden Love down the drive to their car, 'in this case seems to like anyone else.'

Love grunted. 'That woman had a dreadfully haunted look. What do you think is wrong with her?'

'Just frightened.'

'Why?'

Purbright opened the car door. 'There's no knowing at the moment. Probably imaginative and over-wrought. On the other hand, she may actually have seen something that scared her. You'll not get her to talk until she wants to, though. There are women who cling to fear just as some cling to illness. They become quite attached to it.'

Love laid the books on the back seat. 'We'd better make a quick call at the *Citizen* office in case Lintz is still there,' said Purbright. 'We can't very well loot the old man's house without telling his legatee.'

The street door of the *Citizen* was locked, but the office within was brightly lit. Purbright peered through the glass. Behind the advertisement counter—an affair of polished maple and redwood strikingly different from the furnishings of the editorial rooms above—a thin, sandy-haired man sat making entries in a ledger. Hearing the policeman's knock, he raised his head and made helpless gestures meant to convey that the paper's dealings with its public were suspended for the night. Purbright waved back. At last the thin man grudgingly unlocked the door. Yes, Mr Lintz might be upstairs still, but didn't anyone know that newspaper offices had works entrances at the bottoms of alleyways for after-hours contingencies?

Purbright, who did know but had no intention of imperilling his limbs by groping in the dark past bicycles, empty crates and spent paper reels, soothed the man and led Love to the editor's room.

Lintz no longer sat at his desk as though driving an infinitely costly and responsive car. He sat athwart it, surrounded untidily by galley and page proofs.

Love stared at him with innocent admiration. This, he divined, was journalism.

It was, after a fashion, and Lintz was rather tired. Unsmilingly he greeted the two policemen and scrambled down from the sea of council deliberations, smart fines, organs presided at, lucky horseshoes handed, and Dear Sir I hope this catches the eye of . . .

'My, you are busy,' Purbright superfluously informed him. 'You must think it terribly ungracious of us to come worrying you in the middle of all this. Perhaps you'd prefer us to go away until tomorrow?'

'Heavens, no!' said Lintz. 'Let's get it over with now.' He sat down.

'The fact is, there's something here you might be able to help us with.' Purbright beckoned Love, who handed him one of the books. 'It doesn't make much sense to me.'

The editor turned over a couple of pages and looked up quickly. 'This is my uncle's, isn't it?'

'It is, yes. You recognize it?'

'I've seen it in his office at the house. Why have you taken it?'

Purbright gave him a pained look. 'Things have turned out rather unpleasantly, sir; not at all as I would have wished myself. You'll be sorry to learn that we now think Mr Gwill met his death by violence. It will have to be looked into. Probed, you know.'

'Probe' was a word never employed in the generously explicit headlines of the *Citizen*. Lintz suspected Purbright of being sardonic. Be careful, he thought. What he said was: 'You're not serious, surely, inspector?'

Purbright gazed gravely down. 'Oh, yes, I am, Mr Lintz. Very!'

'This is rather dreadful.' There was silence except for the distant clacking of a solitary linotype machine. Lintz turned over the pages of the book of cuttings. 'Why do you think this might have any bearing on what you say has happened?' Caution controlled Lintz's manner like hair oil.

'It may not. I'm only asking your opinion, sir.'

Lintz put on his unilateral smile. 'It so happens that I've been rather puzzled about these myself. I came across them some months ago.'

'Didn't you ask your uncle at the time what they meant?'

'Gracious, no. I knew better than to ask outright about anything. It's obvious what they are, of course. They're small ads from my own paper ("my own" already, thought Purbright), but why he'd collected them is another matter. By the way, does the list of names and addresses at the back of the book mean anything to you?'

'At the back? I saw no list.'

'Yes, here . . .' Lintz shut the book and turned over the back coverboard. The page beneath was blank. 'My mistake. He must have torn it out. That's where it was.'

'You can't remember any of the names, I suppose?'

'No, I only glanced at them once when I was waiting for the old man. I vaguely remember noticing that several of the addresses were down in the Sharms and Haven area.'

'And the advertisements themselves: is there anything peculiar about them?'

Lintz turned to the clippings. 'They're not exactly common or garden offers. Antiques aren't in my line, though.'

'Were they in Mr Gwill's?'

'Not to my knowledge.'

'But they might have been?'

'Look,' said Lintz. 'I think we'd better have House up here. He handles the advertising. Perhaps he knows something about these.'

He left the room and the others heard him call down the staircase. A few moments later he returned with the thin man from the front office.

House scrutinized the cuttings.

'These are all "for sales" that Mr Gwill brought in himself,' he announced. He pointed to the final line of one advertisement. 'You see that box number. It has the letters C.S. in front of it. You'll notice the others have as well. None of the ordinary ads have anything but figures as box references. We used to sort out the replies with C.S. numbers and put them through directly to the boss.'

'Were those his instructions?' Lintz asked.

'They were,' affirmed House, with the air of having settled the matter once and for all.

But Lintz remained inquisitive. 'Where did the copy come from?' he asked.

'From Mr Gwill.'

'Had he prepared it himself, do you know?'

'It was in his writing. Lately it was, anyway.'

'What do you mean by lately?'

'Oh, the past half year or more.'

'But before that it wasn't in his writing?'

'It used to be typed mostly, as far as I can remember.'

Lintz looked at Purbright, inviting him to take over the questioning.

'Now then, Mr House,' the inspector began genially, 'what do you suppose Mr Gwill was putting these advertisements in the paper for? Did you never wonder what they were all about?'

'I thought perhaps he had a friend in the second-hand trade, as you might say.'

'But the friend could have put them in himself, surely. Mr Gwill was a busy man. He wouldn't be likely to go on acting as somebody else's messenger week after week.'

'You'd hardly think so,' House agreed.

'I presume you never saw any of the replies?'

'Me? No, I didn't.'

'Were there many? Incidentally, how often were the adverts put in?'

'Four or five went in at a time most weeks. Sometimes there'd be one or two extra. Each ad brought up to half a dozen replies.'

'The usual number for that kind of advertisement; for antiques, I mean?'

'Well, I can't really say. They were the only ones.'

'You've no idea, Mr House, of who might have been associated with Mr Gwill in placing these advertisements?'

The thin man shook his head.

'When,' asked Purbright, 'was the last batch published?'

House thought for a moment before replying. 'Not last week; we published Tuesday because of Christmas and the ads being light. No, it was the Wednesday before.'

'And there are no replies still in the office?'

'Not now. The boss collected them all on the Thursday and Friday. They always came in very promptly and he never let them be left lying.'

When House had descended to his ledgers once more, Purbright looked thoughtfully at the cuttings. 'When's the latest you can take an advertisement for this week's paper?'

'We print tomorrow. Five o'clock today would have been the deadline in the ordinary way, but I could get something in tomorrow morning, if you like.'

Purbright nodded. 'Good. Now what would you recommend? Sideboards . . . washstands . . . commodes? No, not commodes; we'd better stick to what seem to have been the rules. Let's try some that have been in already. These, eh?' He marked little crosses in pencil against three of the cuttings. 'Perhaps you wouldn't mind making copies, though, Mr Lintz; I'd like to hang on to the book just for the time being.'

Lintz drew over a pad of copy paper and began writing.

When he had finished, he placed the three sheets on a clear corner of the desk. 'Whom shall I charge them to?' he asked.

'Oh, the poor old police, I suppose.' Purbright smiled thoughtfully at Lintz. Then he sighed. 'You'll have gathered,' he said, 'that detection is very much in the air just now, sir. It's rather a novelty, but we'll have to get used to it.'

'Meaning?'

'Meaning in the first place that everyone at all closely connected with your late uncle is going to have to answer some questions—or have them asked, rather. I can see I'm likely to be unpopular, but there it is.'

'You've more questions for me, I presume?' Lintz seemed almost indifferent.

'I'm afraid I have, sir. Would you mind?'

An answer, Lintz opened a drawer of his desk and took out a foolscap sheet. 'You don't need to flannel, inspector. My wife has told me over the phone of your colleague's—your assistant's—call this afternoon. I imagine you want to know where I was until this morning?'

'It would be helpful, sir.'

Lintz handed him the typescript. 'That statement should save time for both of us. You will see from it that after leaving my uncle at his home until getting to bed in my own house beside my own wife, I managed to spend every minute in the company of witnesses.'

Purbright read rapidly through the paper. 'How very thoughtful of you,' he murmured appreciatively. 'I must say I like the last touch, sir.'

Lintz looked at him sharply. 'Oh?'

'Yes, sir. I can't imagine any more respectable midnight occupation than playing chess. And'—Purbright raised one eyebrow—'with an undertaker, of all people.'

CHAPTER SIX

Mr Jonas Bradlaw was, when off duty, as amiable a representative of his craft as you could wish to meet. Undertakers, by and large, are brisk, sanguine, workman-like fellows, and not at all the miserable ghouls mistakenly imagined by those unable to dissociate what they believe to be a dreadful conclusion from the agents charged with its expeditious arrangement. Mr Bradlaw gave such slanderers the lie. He was not gloomy, for he conceived his task to be a useful and rewarding one. He was not cadaverous; half a lifetime of knocking oak and elm into elongated hexagons had given him a solid physique that even now, in the comparative idleness of proprietorial supervision, lent nearly as much dignity to a funeral as had any pair of his late father's black horses. Nor was he a hand-rubbing necrophile; he regretted death in a general way as much as anyone and was sorry when old friends came under his roof in attitudes of stiff formality and desirous no longer of taking part in the conversation.

Conversation—of a lightish kind—he valued, for he was a divorced man (on account of overmuch and carelessly directed amiability, it was said), and led a home life practically devoid of the spoken word. This was because his young housekeepers came and went at such frequent intervals that not one had had time to tire of her employer's television set sufficiently to find anything to say before bed-time. He had once toyed with the idea of getting rid of the set, but had baulked at putting his personal attractions, unaugmented, to the test. Could it be, he had sometimes secretly wondered, that his housekeepers regarded him as a price, not a prize?

On the morning following that on which an unexpected commission for Mr Bradlaw had been found in the field opposite The Aspens, the undertaker moved busily around his yard and workshop, hiding an inner unease with a more than usually jocose encouragement of his three joiners. 'A good board, that, Ben.' 'How's the missus, Charlie? . . . Aye, take the beading over that knot, lad.' 'God, this'n'll twist right off the bloody rollers if there's a ha'porth of damp on Thursday!'

He bustled from bench to trestle in his waistcoat and pinstripes. A wing collar, ready for rapid attachment, hung on a nail above the glue-pot. At the far end of the shop, safe from sawdust and pitch-splashing, was suspended his morning coat. Bradlaw, like a fireman, could be presentable for duty within seconds of a call. Rather pointless, really, he sometimes reflected, was this constant readiness to dash off somewhere. His were the most patient customers in the world. Yet it paid to give the impression of efficiency, concern, dispatch.

He had returned a short time previously from the hospital where, in consideration of Mrs Poole's solitude and nervousness and at the suggestion of Inspector Purbright, the remains of Mr Gwill had been given refrigerated accommodation until the funeral. The coffin was almost ready. It was a nice job. Bradlaw hoped it might to taken into the hospital during visiting hours. One on-the-spot demonstration was worth a whole printing of calendars.

Yet even this prospect did not much lighten Brad-

law's thoughts. The police, he had been told on his
return from the hospital, had called in his absence
and would come back later. And that, he reflected,
could mean only one thing. He looked at his watch.
The inquest would be nearly over. He listened as he
dodged around among the elm shavings for Betty—no,
it was Eileen now—to ring the bell summoning him to
the office.

Eventually the bell did sound. Bradlaw hastily
harnessed himself in the wing collar, hooked around
it the ready-knotted black tie, and wriggled into his
coat as he crossed the yard and entered the house.

Closing the door behind him, he eyed the two waiting men.

'Good morning, gentlemen,' said Bradlaw gravely,
tucking his chin well down and doing his best to convey the impression that he, death's ferryman, had
touched shore for five minutes only, but would consider accepting a message for the other side provided
it was brief, and addressed to the highest authority.

'Hello, there!' responded Purbright. Love winked
cheerfully and perched himself on a chair arm. Bradlaw, who knew and was known by both men perfectly
well, realized that the presumably solemn nature of
their inquiries was not going to prevent them from
treating him with familiarity. Which was a pity, for
his nervousness would have been better concealed if
professional gloom could have been assumed on both
sides.

'Well, here's a fine how-d'ye-do,' began Purbright,
offering cigarettes. 'What do you know about it, Nab?'

Hearing his nickname, Bradlaw abandoned hope of
being able to remain stuffy and safe. But he wasn't
going to be backslapped into parting with anything
compromising. He rolled his head, glanced at the
shut door and hoarsely confided: 'They tell me he
went out and got himself knocked off: is that right?'

Purbright unexpectedly jabbed Bradlaw's paunch. 'Dead right,' he whispered. 'Point is . . . who? Eh?'

'Poor old Gwill.' Bradlaw relaxed. Purbright seemed inclined to be bar-parlourish about the affair, a good sign. 'You'd never have thought he was the sort to end up like that. Here, it wasn't women, was it?' He pronounced 'women' like a medical term.

'Dunno,' Purbright said. 'Might it have been?'

Bradlaw pretended to consider. Then he shook his head. 'I never heard of anything. Mind you, there's often a woman in these things. They're queer creatures. Damn me, they are, you know.'

'There's the woman next door, of course. Had he anything to do with her, would you say?'

Bradlaw looked momentarily shaken. 'Why, have you seen her?'

Watching him, Purbright replied: 'I happened to run into her yesterday. She said she'd been away.'

'Ah!' Bradlaw paused, and added: 'No, she's got her head screwed on. Widows are safe enough as a rule. She'd been away, you said?'

'That's right. Why?'

'You mean, she can't have done it?'

'We haven't decided yet who could and who couldn't. We're at the damn-fool question stage. Let's see'—Purbright eyed Bradlaw with faint amusement— 'what we can find in that line for you, shall we? What, for instance, were you doing on the night before last? And don't say laying in business in Heston Lane.'

'Laying out, sir.'

'You shut up, Sid; I'm waiting for Nab to incriminate himself.'

Bradlaw chuckled and smoothed the few remaining parallel lines of hair across his pinkly shining head. 'Night before last . . .' He massaged the putty of his mouth and frowned. 'Night before last . . .' He removed his hand and his mouth returned to its own devices, the first of which was to ejaculate: 'Buffs!'

'Pardon?' said Purbright.

'Buffs. There was a lodge meeting. Then I popped in at the club. That chap Lintz from the paper—know him?—he was there. I brought him back with me as a matter of fact. Ethel—no, Eileen—made us some supper and he stayed until . . . Oh, I don't know, half-past one or two.'

'Doing what?'

'Heaven knows. Talking. Having a couple of beers. I really can't remember.'

'You wouldn't be playing chess by any chance?'

'Chess? I wouldn't be surprised. Is that what he said?'

'You seem rather vague about it.'

'Not a bit of it. We played chess.' Bradlaw turned to Love and explained: 'It's a sort of complicated draughts, you know.'

'Anyway,' said Purbright, 'you were definitely with Lintz all the time, say, eleven until two?'

'Oh, yes. Except when he was out in the yard, of course.'

'In the yard?'

'He wanted some fresh air, he said. I remember that because he let the door catch and had to wake me up to get in again. Chess,' added Bradlaw feelingly, 'can be bloody tiring.'

'So you don't know how long he was out?'

'Not really. Can't have been long, though. Too cold.'

'Could he have got out of the yard into the street?'

'Into the lane, yes; but why should he?'

'Was his car in the lane?'

'I think so . . . No, we'd come back in the Bedford—my van, you know.' Bradlaw frowned. 'Here, but you're not trying to make out that George nipped out for a jimmy riddle, and then took a fancy to slap down Uncle and got back here before I knew he'd gone?'

Purbright looked at him in silence for several seconds, then smiled. 'Now you see what nasty people your policemen pals can be when they want.'

Bradlaw puffed out his cheeks indignantly.

'What did you know about Gwill?' Purbright resumed.

'Not much. Why?'

'You saw him at his house pretty regularly, didn't you?'

'Now and again.'

'He didn't play chess, I suppose?'

'Gawd, you are in a griping mood. Anyone would think you suspected me.'

'Perish the thought. Why did you go to see him?'

'Just to be sociable. I'm a steady advertiser, too.'

'He didn't give dinner parties for all his advertisers, surely. Who else went with you?'

'Rodney Gloss was there sometimes—his solicitor. Doc Hillyard, too, occasionally. That's all, as far as I remember.'

'What about Harold Carobleat?'

'Well, what about him? He's dead.'

'That's all right. I just wanted a general picture of social life at the Gwills'. We have to start with something, you know.'

Bradlaw shrugged and began tracing numeral outlines on the desk calendar with one finger. 'I'll tell you this much,' he said slowly, 'you needn't waste time looking at Gwill's friends for whoever killed him. I've known him, and them, for a good few years. Look, doctors and lawyers in a place like this don't go round murdering people.'

'Nor undertakers?' murmured Purbright.

'No, not undertakers, either. Why the hell should

they?' Bradlaw seemed to feel a sudden surge of resentment. 'You flounder about and make all sorts of wild insinuations against people just because they knew somebody who's been found dead. Damn it, I don't think you even know yet how the fellow was killed.'

Purbright said patiently: 'No, I don't think we do,' and waited.

'Right; then why go casting around for suspects like . . . like a quizz-master or something?' (Bradlaw went to television for most of his derogatory similes.)

'He's the one,' said Purbright to Love, jerking his thumb at Bradlaw. 'Got the bracelets, Sid? Bracelets,' he explained to the now peeved undertaker, 'are what we call handcuffs. Very slangy.'

Bradlaw grunted, looked at his watch and scowled. 'Come on,' he pleaded. 'I've people coming at twelve. What else do you want to know?'

'Just three more things, Nab, I think. Firstly, what business was Gwill mixed up in apart from his paper?'

'I haven't the faintest idea.'

'Very well. Secondly, if none of his friends had any reason to kill him, who else did?'

Bradlaw shook his head. 'That's your job to find out. I'd be inclined to ask who got anything out of it. But maybe nobody did. I don't know.'

'Lastly, what was Gwill's relationship with Mrs Carobleat?'

'You asked me that before.'

'Not in so many words.'

'I still can't tell you. I only know what people have said, but that doesn't signify. You should hear what some of them have hinted about my housekeeper. A lot of damned spiteful old cows. In this town you even need a chaperone when you go to measure a stiff.'

'How trying for you, Nab.' Purbright picked up his hat and motioned Love to leave with him. 'You must bear up, my friend. Don't give way like poor old Gloss.'

Bradlaw froze in the action of opening the door. He turned. 'What the hell are you getting at?'

Purbright smiled and pushed past him into the street. 'Gloss,' he said, 'is scared—something horrid.' The two policemen moved off in what seemed to Bradlaw slow and ominous companionship.

At the end of the street, Purbright turned the corner and drew Love into a shop doorway some yards further on. 'I'm going back to the station to see what the fellows have picked up from Heston Lane,' he said. 'You hang on here and watch for Nab Bradlaw. I've an idea he'll want to go visiting. If he takes that van of his, it's too bad. He might feel like exercise, though.'

'How long do you want me to stick to him?'

'Only until he goes home again. It's just on twelve now. He said he had some callers, so he'll probably see them first. Don't catch cold.'

Love remained a few minutes looking into the shop window. Then he walked back to the corner. He glanced down Bride Street towards Bradlaw's house, saw no one, and crossed over. For the next quarter of an hour he did his best to make hanging around a deserted road junction on a winter morning look a reasonable occupation.

Eventually he saw a small group leave what he judged to be the undertaker's office and walk away in the opposite direction. Shortly afterwards, a single figure emerged at the same point. As it approached, he recognized Bradlaw and sought another doorway. He gave Bradlaw time to reach the corner. Then carefully he looked out.

Bradlaw, whose walk was distinguishable by a slight roll to the left like the motion of a top-laden boat, had turned off into St Anne's place and was now going away from Love. The sergeant gave him fifty yards' lead and followed, keeping close to the shops on his left.

Several people were now between them, but Love had no difficulty in keeping the rhythmically listing figure of the undertaker in sight until, quite suddenly, it peeled off, mounted a short flight of railed steps, and disappeared.

Love slowed his pace and crossed the road. From the other side he could see only two doorways with steps. He strolled slowly until he was opposite the first. The door was closed. The second entrance was not. He concluded that it must have been through there that Bradlaw had passed.

He crossed over again and continued in the same direction, noting the names on the brass plates outside the second door. Then he became interested in shop windows once more and tried to forget how cold his feet were getting.

Nearly half an hour went by.

At last Bradlaw emerged. Love, at that moment twenty yards away, prepared to follow him again. He came nearer and tried to see which direction the undertaker had chosen. But there was no sign of him.

Love crossed the road carefully, craning his neck and rising on tip-toe to see over the intervening citizenry. It was only when a second man appeared at the top of the steps and hurried down to the kerb that Love realized what had happened.

He ran forward in time to see the car draw away

and accelerate towards the town centre. The passenger was Bradlaw. The driver, whom Love recognized when he glanced swiftly behind him before letting out the clutch, was Mr Rodney Gloss.

CHAPTER SEVEN

Detective constables Harper and Pook had spent the morning calling from door to door in Heston Lane, an occupation only a little less dispiriting then Love's patrol of the chilling flagstones of St Anne's Place. Every now and then, Harper (even numbers) would meet or be met by Pook (odd numbers) and compare notes on the remarkable blindness and defective hearing of the residents.

'Dead stupid, these people,' opined Harper, with dismal regularity.

'God, what a lot!' responded Pook.

It did not strike them as at all reasonable that a murder could have been committed so privately as to have escaped entirely the notice of upwards of sixty householders, most of them patently inquisitive insomniacs with a keen sense of the significance of every passing footstep and every distantly slammed door.

'They must know something,' Harper declared.

'Scared we'll ask for their dog licence,' theorized Pook.

They parted once more for odd and even investigation, like vacuum cleaner salesmen doggedly canvassing a community served by gas.

About half-way through the morning, Pook discovered he was far ahead of the last point at which he had seen Harper march up a driveway. Perhaps the lucky devil had found a house where hot coffee and reminiscences of a son's career in the North-West Frontier Police were waiting. Pook noted the number of his next call and strolled back. Harper, he saw, was just coming out of the house, looking at his notebook and apparently confirming something with a tubby, beady-eyed and garrulous woman who nodded energetically and pointed occasionally in the direction of The Aspens, whence the detective had been working their hitherto unproductive way.

'That one was a bit more useful,' said Harper as he rejoined his colleague.

'Coffee?' asked Pook, enviously.

'Tea,' absently replied Harper, 'I think.' He gave a final glance at his notebook and slipped it in his pocket.

Pook grunted and looked back sadly at the long line of odd and tea-less residences at whose doors he had knocked or rung in vain. 'We'd better do the rest,' he said. 'By the way, did you get anything out of her—apart from a cuppa?'

'Three, actually,' Harper corrected. 'And a list of people who could have been at Gwill's place after midnight.'

Worse and worse. Pook stared at him. 'Don't talk wet. These people all sink into a coma round about eight. She probably made something up because she was sorry for you.'

'Oh, no.' Harper was pleased and brisk. 'It so happens her daughter was out at a dance or something and the old woman was so scared she'd come back ruined that every time she heard anyone coming from town she popped down to the gate to see if it was girlie. Hence the who's who. She didn't know them all, but I've four names and a few descriptions.'

The inquisition was resumed. But the houses here were much nearer the town. The detectives' automatic catechism drew no more information that seemed to have any bearing on what had happened at or near The Aspens. Pook was reduced to putting down in his notebook an account of the narrow escape of one old woman's cat from death beneath the wheels of a black van driven 'furiously and without the slightest regard for animals' from the direction of Flaxborough at half an hour past midnight. 'I noticed specially because it came back again later, officer, and poor Winston called out from the kitchen—well, they *know*, don't they?'

It was at Winston's home that Pook's fast was ended. But his benefactor was still so upset that she very nearly poured him a saucer of milk before it occured to her that he might prefer tea.

Love found Purbright digesting, like a sleepy boa constrictor, the offerings of Harper and Pook. He added his own news that Bradlaw had called upon lawyer Gloss and been driven off by him in his car. This was accepted by the inspector with a mild 'Did he now?'

'Anything new?' asked Love.

'Oh, bits and pieces. They may make sense eventually. Unfortunately we're still at the stage of not knowing what to throw away. Harper's just unloaded this lot, for instance. "Middle-aged man with stick, carrying case and looking at numbers on gates . . . girl in hurry wearing dark fur-trimmed coat and high-heeled shoes . . . Maurice Hoylake, garage proprietor, on bicycle . . . man, fairly well-off looking, with trilby hat and small feet . . . Dr Hillyard, general practitioner, of Flaxborough . . . Mr William Semple . . . man in raincoat, rather drunk . . . Miss Peabody, millinery assistant and amateur dramatics secretary . . ." And from Pook, with apologies and stiff-lipped readiness for further foolish errands, "One black van, driven to the danger of cats up and down Heston Lane all of a Monday midnight-O".'

'And what are they supposed to mean?'

'They are the fruits of inquiries by Messrs Harper and Pook of the residents of Heston Lane. A list of everyone seen in those parts around the time that Gwill was likely to have been murdered. They'll all need to be questioned when we can get round to it, but at the moment, it's the last name that rings the loudest bell, isn't it?'

'Hillyard?'

'Yes. Do you know him, by the way?'

'I've never actually met him. He's a bottle-hitter, from what I hear.'

'It seems so. He turned up while I was talking to the Carobleat woman yesterday afternoon. She knew him well enough to dislike him, and I'd say he's not over fond of her. Wherever he was going on Monday night, I doubt if it was to an assignation with Mrs Carobleat.'

'You'll tackle him about Monday?'

'Naturally. It might not be easy, though. When he's sober, which may not be very often, he's probably well fortified with professional dignity and Gaelic awkwardness. And when he's drunk, I expect he becomes a mystic, which will be a damn sight worse.'

Purbright looked again at his notes. 'What do you make of the "well-off looking man with trilby hat and small feet"? Small feet . . . what a curious thing for anyone to notice at that time of night.'

'Not necessarily. When I used to be on nights I could tell some people by their feet. It's the way they walk and the amount of noise they make. Those with little feet look rather like those prancy characters of Edward Lear—you know, walking on points.'

Purbright regarded him with admiration. 'Sid, you read books!'

Love beamed. 'I'm jolly well educated,' he retorted cheerfully. 'I can detect, too. Roddy Gloss walks like one of Mr Lear's Old Men Of.'

The telephone forestalled Purbright's reply. It was Lintz. He had just realized, apparently, that his uncle's end was the beginning of a news story that was likely to run a course quite independent of his own feelings in the matter. He had toyed with, but finally abandoned, the idea of announcing the death in simple "We regret . . ." terms designed to give the impression that Gwill had expired unaided and in an orthodox manner, and now wished to know if he could give instructions for the local account of the affair to include an official statement from the police.

Purbright pondered. He had quickly learned to meet the bright, hungry questions of men who called him "Old Boy" and seemed passionately interested in irrelevancies, with a noncommittal geniality that they were pleased to take as confirmation of everything they asked. But the *Citizen* might prove useful. Unlike the Nationals, whose touching faith in their readers' readiness to believe absolutely anything was so misplaced, a local weekly commanded credence.

'Look, Mr Lintz,' said Purbright, 'you can use all the facts as I believe you know them already. I'd like you to add this, though. Say the police are anxious to hear from anyone who was out in the Heston Lane area on Monday night from eleven-thirty onwards. Oh, and you might add a mention of a plain, black van. We'd like a word with the driver. . . . Yes, same place, Heston Lane; it went up from town just before twelve and turned about half an hour later. Pardon? Yes, black. . . . That's very good of you, sir.'

He grinned as he replaced the phone. 'I was won-

dering how to put the wind up Lintz. That might
have done it.'

'The bit about the van?'

'Yes. How many plain black vans would you say
there are in Flaxborough?'

'There's ours.'

'Don't be fatuous.'

Love thought a moment. 'There can't be more than
a couple of others. Bradlaw's is black, isn't it?'

'It is. Now what did you make of his story this
morning?'

'Thin.'

'Very. I rather fancy, d'you know, that Bradlaw and
Lintz cooked it up beforehand at Nab's instigation.
He certainly took Lintz home with him—I've checked
on that. Since the murder, he could have rubbed it
into Lintz that as Gwill's heir he was bound to be suspected, and given him to believe that he, Bradlaw,
would provide his alibi. But Nab was smart enough
this morning to leave a hole in his story—the part
about Lintz going out into the yard. It was deliberately added for our benefit. And for Bradlaw's. It was
the surest way of putting Lintz under suspicion. You
noticed how Nab implied that he'd had a good deal
to drink? The air of uncertainty about the game of
chess . . . the suggestion that he had dropped off
to sleep and wouldn't have known how long Lintz
was away . . . he did it all very nicely.'

'Don't you think you're giving him too much credit
for cunning? We don't know for certain that either of
them left the house.'

'There's the report of the van.'

'Just passing through from some other town, perhaps.'

'Don't forget it came back again.'

'True.'

'Incidentally,' Purbright went on, 'just before you

came in I rang the Unionist Club and had a word with Hubbard, the steward. He confirmed what I'd suspected. Nab can drink all night and still see the sixteenths of that foot rule of his. Lintz pewks on a pint. On Monday night he picked his way out like a deep sea diver. Nab was cold sober and steering him.'

Love looked impressed. 'In that case, it's possible that it was Bradlaw who knew what was going to happen and who felt in need of an alibi.'

'Quite possible. But suppose we can prove that Nab took his van and drove to Heston Lane end and back. We still have no notion of why he should have wanted to murder Gwill. He can't be so short of work that he has to provide it for himself. We still don't know how it was done. And we don't know who else might have been involved; heaving the body around was too much for one, surely.'

'Hillyard was seen going that way. But I suppose he could have been visiting a patient.'

'What, on foot?'

'No, perhaps not.'

Purbright rubbed his cheek. 'We can't stretch coincidence three ways. Hillyard was identified. Someone resembling the nimble Mr Gloss was described. And a van very like Nab Bradlaw's was spotted. All around the same time and bound in the same direction. All three were friends of the murderee. One is now frightened and a second produces a leaky alibi, while the third breathes whisky fumes and gives portentous Caledonian grunts. Pray heaven we're not faced with a conspiracy, Sid. Conspiracies are the most dreadful things to sort out. Oh, God, they're maddening, believe me. . . .'

The telephone rang. Again it was Lintz. The inspector would remember the instruction to insert three advertisements in that week's issue on the lines of he knew what? Yes, well, it had turned out that four insertions had been ordered by Gwill himself the previous Saturday. Mr House had just seen them in proof. He hadn't known about them before because the girl had taken them while he was out of the office. What did the inspector want done now?

'Oh,' said Purbright, 'cancel mine and let the original ones go in. So much the better, sir. And thanks for letting me know. While we're on the subject, I'd be obliged if you would make certain of being given all the replies yourself as they come in. Don't allow them out of your hands, sir. I think that may be important. You what? . . . Yes, telephone my office here as soon as anything arrives—the very first one—and I'll come over.'

Love watched him replace the receiver and said: 'It could be, couldn't it, that you're taking a risk with that chap. How do you know he won't grab the replies and hand you some he's concocted himself?'

'I don't. But I can hardly impound the whole newspaper and staff it with our lads, can I? This is just one of those occasions when we have to take a chance on somebody.'

'There may be nothing in this advertisement business.'

'Quite. We shall probably know by the week-end. Incidentally, I thought the inquest went reasonably well, didn't you?'

Love agreed that it had. Whatever Mr Chubb had done to prime Flaxborough's irascible and senile Coroner, it had achieved remarkable results. Not only had Mr Amblesby forborne from interrupting the medical evidence of Dr Heineman with malicious cross-questioning about his origins, but he had made no attempt to introduce homilies on drink, gadgets, Edwardian levees, or the monstrous prodigality of the working class, all subjects which Mr Amblesby considered very proper to inquests.

The only dangerous moment had been when Lintz, giving evidence of identification, touched upon his having left Gwill alone at his house on the evening before the discovery of the body. The Coroner, malevolently clicking his dentures and fixing Lintz with an eye like an agate dipped in sputum, accused: 'Do you mean to tell me you left an old gentleman of his age on his own and with no one to look after him?' Lintz sullenly retorted that his uncle had been perfectly capable, by no means elderly, and strongly opposed to being looked after by anybody. 'But he must be over ninety,' persisted Mr Amblesby. 'He was on the association committee with me when Sir Philip trounced that radical chap . . . Malley, what was the fellow's name? Pro-Boer, he was . . .' The sergeant had thereupon nursed him back into the present with an explanation that Marcus Gwill's father was not the gentleman with whom they were now concerned. The rest of the proceedings had gone smoothly enough, with Mr Amblesby harmlessly slumped in a reminiscent coma.

After lunch, Purbright took himself off through the fog that was spreading inland from the already obscured harbour district and sought the offices of Possett, Gloss and Weatherby.

Mr Gloss, who privately regarded inspectors of police much as the managing director of a public transport company might regard inspectors of tickets, was careful nevertheless to give his welcome that air of unpatronizing amiability that so effectively discourages subordinates from putting demands or awkward questions. He waved Purbright to a chair, then took a seat—a smaller, harder one than his visitor's—beside, but not at, his desk. He offered him a cigarette, a Woodbine, lit it for him with a match and said melifluously and invitingly: 'Now, Inspector.'

'Now, sir,' responded Purbright, with a smile of

such friendliness that if he had said outright that here was a game two could play Gloss could have taken his meaning more clearly. 'You'll have some idea of what I'm after, I expect?'

Gloss also smiled. 'Your intention, doubtless, is to grill me, inspector,' he said good-humouredly. 'That is, assuming that you are investigating the lamentable death of my client, Mr Gwill.'

'You were his legal adviser, I understand, sir?'

'I was, indeed. And am still, so far as the posthumous disposition of his affairs is concerned.'

'He made a will, I suppose?'

'Oh, yes. A straightforward document. Everything goes to his nephew, Mr Lintz, including the controlling interest in the Flaxborough Citizen Printing and Publishing Company. I believe the arrangement was fairly widely understood, so there can be no harm in my revealing the terms of the will. The fact is that Mr Gwill had no one else to whom he could leave his possessions: no one of blood relationship, that is.'

Gloss looked at Purbright intently, as if daring him to cross-examine. But the will seemed to have lost significance already. The inspector went straight on to other matters.

'How long had you known Mr Gwill, sir?'

'A fair number of years, I should say. Almost a lifetime, in fact. The professional relationship dates back to, oh, the early 'thirties.'

'You had always been on good terms with him?'

'Come, inspector; you do not, surely, expect me to make any such claim?' Gloss was the bluff and open advocate now. 'We had differences of opinion on many occasions. Marcus was not of an altogether amenable disposition. One made allowances . . .' He shrugged. 'One got on, notwithstanding. I wonder your inquiries, even at their present presumably undeveloped stage, have not adduced evidence of a certain coolness in my client's attitude to others.

'But'—Gloss bulged his eyes—'do not misunderstand me. At no time, no time, was there any serious likelihood of a breach between us. Men of business never allow temporary emotional discord to blind them to the mutual advantages of association. Please do not regard that as cynical, inspector; it is plain truth.'

'It sounds logical, sir. May I ask if you had any business interest in common with Mr Gwill beyond the . . . the normal client-solicitor relationship?'

'Pray amplify that question, inspector. I am not altogether with you.'

'Perhaps I had better put it another way. Are you aware of any occupation, any source of income, of Mr Gwill's, apart from his ownership of the newspaper?'

'Ah, now you are framing the question very differently. In its original form, it almost implied suspicion that Gwill and I might have shared in some pecuniary enterprise on the side, as it were. I do hope you entertain no thought of the possibility of anything so improper?'

'I'm sure you would be guilty of nothing the Law Society might frown on, Mr Gloss.'

'No, indeed. That would be quite unrealistic. As to your amended question, now . . .' Gloss puckered his brow and was silent a while. Then he shook his head. 'The answer must be no, inspector. Not that the bare negative is incapable of qualification, you understand; but I think it will serve in the context of police investigation.'

'If I were of an uncharitable disposition,' Purbright said quietly, 'I might almost take that to be a roundabout way of saying that your client's sudden departure has left some money lying around that isn't strictly accounted for.'

Gloss looked at the policeman with undisguised admiration. 'Upon my soul, but you're a perceptive fellow, inspector. And you're absolutely right. The trouble is, you know'—he leaned forward—'that my client suffered a disadvantage common to many gentlemen in a commercial way of occupation. They are naturally concerned to order their affairs to meet the contingencies of our times. Taxation and so forth, you understand. But such arrangements demand supervision by a live principal—a man who can sign his name—perhaps several names, alas. Manipulation is called for, inspector. Manipulation. And a corpse, God bless us, cannot manipulate.'

'I see what you mean, sir.'

The solicitor crossed one leg over the other and examined a carefully polished shoe cap. 'You must not conclude, of course, that any substantial proportion of Mr Gwill's assets is, how shall we say, frozen. His less orthodox accounts and holdings may need to remain outside the scope of the will for the time being, but they represent no part of the money that has accrued from his publishing business.'

'Can you tell me what they do represent?'

After the briefest of pauses, Gloss shook his head. 'No, inspector, I'm afraid I cannot help you there.'

'You appreciate, I expect, sir, that the fact of Mr Gwill having been murdered obliges us to examine everything about his affairs that might show a motive.'

'Do I take it that you infer from the existence of an unofficial source of income that he might have been obtaining money by exerting pressure on some person?'

'I infer the possibility of blackmail.'

Gloss pursed his lips. 'That is what I imagined might be your line of reasoning. But do you think that if that had been the case my client would have acquainted me with the extent of his investments? He need not have done so.'

'Nor need you have said anything about them to me, sir.'

'No, but I think it safer that I should.'

'Safer? Safer for whom, Mr Gloss?'

'For myself, inspector. I shall be entirely frank with you. It is my private belief that this money was obtained not by blackmail but by other means of questionable legality. What they were I do not know and I do not wish to know. But some months ago I noticed a change in the man's manner. He became more excited, yet there was an element of fear in his excitement. He boasted of the supplements to his means and hinted at his having to be clever to obtain them. The sums themselves, as far as I have been able to check, were not spectacular. I think it was the method of coming by them that gave him some sort of stimulus. I further received the impression that some third person was being deprived of a share in the gains and that his discomfiture was contributing to my client's sense of elation.'

'You felt Gwill was doing something dangerous, you mean? For the thrill of it?'

'Exactly. These little extras had been coming his way for a fairly considerable time, but he had said nothing about them to me, apart from asking advice on investment occasionally.'

'Which you gave?' Purbright interjected.

'Oh, yes. Why not? I had no proof of my client's transactions being in any way improper.'

'Please go on, sir.'

'Well, during recent months he grew more loquacious. Not factually informative, you understand, but full of little hints and boasts of a slightly provocative character. He seemed anxious that I should feel involved in some way. I remember he said once that I should need to be careful for my own skin—that was how he put it—for my own skin, if anything happened to him. I asked him what he meant and he said something to the effect that he had made an enemy "good enough for us both". To be quite honest, I had come by that time to suspect my client of being considerably overwrought and perhaps lacking balance.'

'You think now there may have been something in what he said?'

Gloss got up and walked to the window. With his back to Purbright, he went on talking as he stared out at the passing traffic.

'I am inclined to the view,' he said, 'that Gwill said what he did after having conveyed for reasons best known to himself a false impression of our relationship to some other person. This hypothetical third party, it may be, was fobbed off with the story that I had been given custody of monies of which he had been deprived, in order that he would make no direct or violent attempt to recover them from Gwill himself. As things have turned out, it appears that the ruse did not save Gwill from the revenge of the person he had provoked. But what very naturally concerns me, inspector, is that someone who has shown himself capable of murder is now at large and possibly obsessed with the notion that only I now stand between him and what he considers his due.'

At the end of this speech, Gloss turned slowly from the window and stood facing Purbright. 'I trust,' he said, 'you will now appreciate why I made the request—of which your Chief Constable has doubtless acquainted you—for police protection; and why I have disclosed to you what would normally be regarded as professionally confidential matters.'

Purbright rubbed his chin and sighed. He found

the ponderous rectitude of Gloss's recital tiring and an obstacle to his selection of suggestive facts.

'I wonder,' he said at last, 'if you would care to tell me where you were on Monday night, Mr Gloss?'

The sudden change of subject seemed to set the solicitor thumbing hastily through some mental brief. 'Monday night . . . Monday . . .'

'Yes. The night Gwill was killed.'

'Ah . . .' The court manner was returning. Some surprising revelation, clinching a case, confounding a prosecutor, vindicating a wronged client, was about to be tossed, with studied carelessness, before the bench. 'Curiously enough, inspector'—Gloss slowly lowered himself back into his chair and gazed earnestly over interlaced fingers held just above his chin—'I spent Monday evening at the home of Marcus Gwill and stayed until after he was dead.'

CHAPTER EIGHT

'I suppose you would think me facetious if I were to ask if you killed him,' Purbright said.

'Not at all: the question is a proper one in the circumstances,' Gloss conceded. 'But I'm afraid my answer will not help you very much. It is no.'

Purbright took out a notebook. 'I'm my own secretary today,' he remarked wryly. 'I hope you won't be put off by feeling sorry for me, but I really must take a statement after what you've just said.'

'Naturally. I have given the matter some thought and I feel that to give a frank account of what I know of the events of the other evening is the least I can do for the sake of my late client and'—Purbright looked up in time to see a man-of-the-world shrug—'of others.'

'Yourself included, sir?'

'Of course.'

'And Jonas Bradlaw?'

Gloss held up his hand. 'You must not anticipate my statement, inspector.' He looked at his watch and listened. Above the muffled sounds of traffic, a horn sounded briefly. A ship's siren moaned in the estuary beyond Flaxborough dock. There was a light step to the door, a knock, and a plump, spotty girl edged her way in with a tray. Gloss put away his watch and beamed a quick, unmeant smile at her. 'Promptitude,' he said to Purbright when she had gone, 'is one of the qualities most difficult to inculcate into one's office staff today.'

Purbright grunted and put his cup on the desk beside him. He opened the notebook and looked expectantly at the solicitor, who took a sip of his tea and began slowly to dictate.

'Rather late on Monday night—it must have been approximately eleven-thirty—I left my home and walked to the house of Mr Marcus Gwill. I do not normally retire to bed early and a stroll about midnight is not an uncommon exercise for me, so you must not imagine that there was anything extraordinary in my being abroad on that particular night. I do not pretend, however, that the visit to Gwill was in response to a mere whim. He had telephoned me a short time previously and intimated that there was a matter of some urgency he wished to discuss.

'I recall nothing noteworthy about my walk along Heston Lane. I met no one I recognized, although there were several people about who might conceivably have recognized me. It would be about a quarter to twelve when I arrived.

'Another acquaintance of Gwill's was already there. I say acquaintance; actually it was his doctor, the Scotsman Hillyard, whom you probably know. Like myself, he stood in a somewhat closer relationship to Gwill than a purely professional one. When I found him in the drawing-room, I concluded that some sort of a conference was intended, although Gwill had not explained over the telephone what he had in mind. I did not suppose the occasion to be of a purely social nature.'

Gloss paused to look at Purbright's lightly pencilled shorthand worming between the lines. 'Please tell me,' he said, 'if I am forging too far ahead of that admirable squiggle.'

'Not at all, sir,' said Purbright, evenly. 'My squiggle

likes a fleet quarry. But I should like my cup of tea now, if you don't mind.' And he drank it. 'Will you go on from "social nature", sir?'

Gloss frowned, then smoothly resumed.

'Hillyard was seated by the fire and drinking a glass of whisky. He appeared contemplative. Gwill fetched a glass for me and invited me to help myself from the decanter. He took nothing to drink himself; he was an abstainer, you know. I noticed he was chewing, however, and I remember feeling a little irritated at the sight of his jaws working away. Adult sweet-eaters invariably annoy me. They seem furtively self-indulgent and sensual in a horrid, immature way. I mention the fact of Gwill's chewing because it explains why I can tell you very little of something that occurred almost immediately after my arrival, something which I think now may have been of significance.

'The telephone rang, and Gwill took the call in the room where we were sitting. As he listened, he put another loathsome sweetmeat into his mouth, and I was so preoccupied with the way his mastication moved the telephone earpiece up and down that I failed to take any notice of the conversation. There was no doubt of its outcome, though, for Gwill put the instrument down and hastened out of the house with no more than a mumble about being back in a few minutes.'

Gloss paused, then looked very solemnly at Purbright. 'He did not come back and I never saw him again. Hillyard and I waited for perhaps half an hour. Then I went upstairs to ask Mrs Poole if she had any idea of where he might have gone and to request her to remain awake until his return. She was not there, of course. Hillyard and I could think of nothing practical to do in the circumstances and so left the house and walked to our respective homes.'

Purbright glanced up. 'Did you lock the door of the house, sir?'

'We decided it would be better to leave it insecure than to risk his having taken no key and being obliged to break a window or something of that kind.'

'You felt no anxiety on his behalf other than being worried about locking him out?'

'None. Why should we? As a matter of fact, we both took it for granted that he was visiting some house fairly close at hand. It was only later that I realized the unlikelihood of that having been the case.'

'What led you to realize that?'

'I remembered two things about the telephone call that did not register on my mind at the time but which must have made a subconscious impression.'

'Yes, Mr Gloss?'

'Perhaps a minute before the telephone bell rang, I heard a vehicle draw up in the road outside. It has occurred to me since that a public telephone kiosk stands on Heston Lane some little way nearer the town and on the opposite side of the road. I incline to the belief that the call to Gwill's house came from that kiosk and was made by the driver of the vehicle I heard.'

'Can you say what sort of a vehicle it sounded to be, sir?'

'I'm afraid I cannot. It made a noticeable noise, so it is likely to have been a moderately large car or a small lorry.'

'Might it have been a van?'

Gloss considered. 'Conceivably,' he said.

'And now, sir, perhaps you'll tell me the second thing about the telephone call that has come back to you since Monday night.'

'Oh, yes; the second thing.' Gloss's gaze fell; he drummed fingers on his knee and gave, Purbright thought, a fair impersonation of reluctant prosecutor.

'I am almost certain,' he said, 'that Gwill addressed the maker of the telephone call as George.'

'George?'

'That is my recollection, inspector. But I wish to be perfectly fair. My attention, as I have said, was distracted. It is just possible that the name was something similar.'

'Surely there aren't many names that sound similar to George, Mr Gloss?'

'No? No, perhaps not. I have not given the matter much thought. I wished only to be frank and to impart impressions as they have come to me, quite undisturbed by conjecture.'

'Ah, very proper, sir.' The inspector's face was blank. So was the other's. They remained a while looking at each other in querulous politeness. Purbright broke the silence.

'Why did Mr Bradlaw come to see you this morning?'

'Bradlaw . . .' Gloss smiled. 'You had made him nervous, I think. He came here to seek reassurance.'

'Why should he have been nervous?'

'He is inclined to be more sensitive to questioning than you might imagine, inspector. He has a rough manner, but that is deceptive. The troubles of others upset him to a greater extent than is healthy, perhaps, for one in his profession.'

'I have known Mr Bradlaw for quite a few years, sir.'

'Then you will be acquainted with his, ah, idiosyncracies.'

'Yes, I am.'

Gloss nodded and stared up at the ceiling.

'Tell me,' said Purbright in a brisker tone, 'was Bradlaw at Mr Gwill's house at any time on Monday night?'

Without lowering his eyes, Gloss said gently: 'He

may have been. But of course he was not present while I was there—as you must have judged from the fact that I made no mention of him in my account of what transpired.'

Purbright gave a little bow of acknowledgement. Then he asked: 'Did you notice if Mr Gwill took a bucket or a can of water down the drive that night?'

For the first time in the interview the solicitor looked surprised. 'Water? What on earth would he have been doing with buckets of water?'

'What, indeed,' said Purbright, watching him. The bewilderment seemed genuine. Then Gloss's expression changed. 'Wait a moment,' he said, 'I still fail to see the significance of your allusion to water-cans, but I do remember now something that struck me as slightly out of the ordinary when I arrived at Gwill's house. On opening the gate, I noticed the gravel felt sodden underfoot as though heavy rain had fallen. But there had been no rain, of course. And the ground was wet only at that one point.'

'Near the gate?'

'Yes. Just inside, I should say.'

Purbright looked at his watch, stood up, and began buttoning his coat. 'I'm most obliged to you, Mr Gloss; you've been very patient. I do believe I've run out of questions.'

'And I'm not at all sure,' replied Gloss with a court-room smile, 'but that I have run out of answers.'

While Gloss was carefully contributing to Purbright's mounting collecting of enigmas, contradictions, deductions and doubts, two other professional men of Flaxborough were discussing.

Said Mr Bradlaw to Dr Hillyard (with whom he had lately lunched and who now sat regarding him mournfully in his spacious but musty drawing-room):

'The whole damned thing will have to be dropped
for the time being. We can build it up later when the
fuss about poor old Marcus has died down.'

Said Dr Hillyard, self-consciously sober and liver-
ishly emphatic: 'It cannot and needn't. Get that into
your head, man. Marcus asked for what he got, by
God he did, but it can't be left at that. What's running smoothly now will have to keep on running or
else be abandoned altogether. And I'll not see that
happen after what we've put into it.'

'But the police . . .'

'The police! Aye, and what will they do? Run
round in ever-decreasing circles until they become
their own colonic stoppages.' Hillyard stretched out a
lanky leg and kicked at coal at the fire edge. He
scowled at the upsurge of flame.

'Listen,' said Bradlaw, 'I know the man Purbright.
He may not be brilliant but he perseveres. He makes
himself a thorough nuisance and rubs it in by con-
stantly apologizing. I had him to put up with this
morning. I tell you he'll be on our backs until king-
dom come, with his "I hate to trouble you" and
"Mightn't it be so" and "Perhaps you'd care to tell
me".'

'Nonsense. He's just a provincial copper, dig-dig-
ging into what he doesn't understand and hoping for
good luck to save his reputation in the eyes of that
timid old goat of a Chief Constable. He knows nothing
and he'll find nothing. Always provided'—Hillyard's
cheek twitched in the firelight—'that you and I and
friend Gloss remain helpfully obscure and unproduct-
ively cooperative.'

Bradlaw grunted. 'Roddy Gloss is just a shade too
clever sometimes. Keeping up with him can be
dodgy.'

'Never mind that. He'll not take any risks. And
he'll have the sense not to lead you into any.'

'I don't know what you mean by risk if you think he's not asking for trouble by the line he's given old Chubb. You realize what he's going to tell Purbright as soon as he's questioned? Which he will be. Even if it hasn't happened already.'

'Stop talking in bursts, and stop frightening yourself like an old woman. Damn me if you thrombosis fatties aren't all the same.'

Bradlaw, peeved, sat up in his chair. Hillyard took no notice of him but glowered at his own outstretched feet and said slowly: 'We seem to have got away from the main point again, don't we?'

'Eh?'

Hillyard felt in his pocket and drew out a battered cigarette. This he lit with a strip of paper that he tore methodically from the margin of one of the medical journals scattered on the floor by his chair. Quietly, almost sadly, he said: 'There's only one way we can find him.'

'You'll not get it out of her.'

'I don't propose to try any more.'

'Well, then . . .'

'Listen. A patient of mine—one of the more grateful ones—works at the telephone exchange . . .'

Hillyard spoke gently and without banter now. Bradlaw, nervous and doubtful, tried to look intelligent.

Behind the change in the manner of each lay common recognition of the need to be serious and to waste no time. Fear perched in the room.

CHAPTER NINE

The photograph that Purbright pushed across his desk to Love was an enlargement of a hand. The sergeant gave un involuntary jump. A hand, disconnected and twice life-size, can be a startling exhibit when unexpectedly revealed to a man preoccupied with nothing more sinister than desire for an early tea.

Love stared obligingly at the picture.

'Well?' asked Purbright.

Love turned the photograph sideways, then upside down. 'Fine prints old Hastings gets,' he remarked.

Purbright was patient. 'What do you make of the flower? There, look.' He leaned over and traced faint lines, broken but forming part of a general symmetry over the main area of the open palm. They were suggestive of a formalized daffodil.

'The burns?' said Love.

'Yes.'

'They show the shape of what he must have grabbed, I suppose.'

'Correct.'

'So when we find a metal object of the same shape and size that could have been connected to the mains or a cable last Monday night, we'll be a fair way towards knowing how and where old Gwill was done.'

Purbright beamed as if upon a favourite pupil. 'You are sharp today, Sid. I think we might make the best of it and go detecting, don't you?'

The lugubrious Mrs Poole admitted them to The Aspens with the air of a landlady opening the door for lodgers who had forgotten their keys. She seemed resigned to the prospect of the police dropping in and out for the rest of her life, which, judging from her aspect, she had no desire to be prolonged.

Purbright showed her a sketch of the marks on the photographed hand. He did not say what they were, but asked if she could think of any metal object about the house of which the sketch reminded her.

She stared at the drawing, moving her head to one side, then the other. 'I've seen something like it,' she murmured, 'but where, I can't think.'

'Outside, perhaps?' Purbright prompted.

She shook her head. 'You see carvings like that on church pews sometimes. But you said metal, didn't you? Brass or iron, that would be. What about bedsteads, then?'

'Bedsteads?'

'Yes. The old-fashioned ones, you know. There are things like that on some of those I've seen. Like flowers between the rails at the head and foot.' She handed back the piece of paper.

Purbright asked her: 'Is there a bedstead of that kind here?'

'Only mine, sir,' said Mrs Poole, 'but truth to tell I can't remember offhand what the metal parts of it are like, except for the knobs, of course, and not all of them are still there. You'd better come and see.'

But upon Mrs Poole's gaunt bed rails there was no decoration at all, save one large and tarnished brass ball. 'It's funny how you can sleep on something for years and not really notice what it looks like,' she said, modestly thrusting a forgotten corset out of sight.

Purbright stared carefully round the room. It contained no daffodils of iron or of anything else. 'Perhaps we'd better take a quick look into the other rooms, now that we're here—if that wouldn't inconvenience you, Mrs Poole.'

That was all right, she assured him. Having seen to her own little night-box of privacy being closed up snug and naptha-scented once again, she left them and descended to whatever forlorn tasks she still found to do in the deserted house.

The two policemen looked into all the other upstairs rooms. Only the two largest bedrooms were furnished. Both their beds were of wood. Of metal-work there was no trace, except for one gas bracket that had been left for some obscure reason sprouting from a landing wall like a dead and dusty plant.

Purbright watched for power points. There was one in each of the large bedrooms and three more along the corridor and landings. He examined each carefully. All had a thick film of dust around the sockets.

They continued the search downstairs. It revealed nothing suggestive apart from four more power points, three of them dusty, and a roll of wire in the meter cupboard. Love tugged at this expertly and shook his head. 'Bell wire—no use for mains,' he said.

They halted in the study-like room and stared out into the garden, with it's dripping laurels. The house around them seemed damp and secretive and sorry for itself. 'We'll get nothing more here, I doubt,' said Purbright.

'Do you believe Gloss's story?' Love asked him.

'Up to a point. I think they were all here that night. Gwill and Gloss and Hillyard and Bradlaw.'

'Bradlaw, too?'

'I'd be much surprised if he wasn't. They were in something or other together and on Monday night there must have been a development of such importance to all of them that a conference of some kind became necessary. Either that, or else the other three came here by arrangement among themselves to put Gwill out of the way.'

'Electrocution seems an uncertain way of going about it.'

'Not at all. If only you can make sure your victim is nicely earthed—in a bath is the classic position—a shot of ordinary mains current is just as effective as a cannon ball.'

'You think he was actually killed here, then?'

'It's the most likely place if there was a conspiracy.'

'If he was murdered here,' said Love, 'they all must have been concerned to some extent. One of them could hardly have knocked him off without the others being aware of it. And it would have taken more than one man to carry the body over to the field afterwards.'

Purbright frowned. 'There's something queer about the story of the man Gloss. He mentioned Gwill's having been eating up to the time of leaving the house. We know that to be correct. It lends strength to his tale, great strength. Had Gwill been murdered here by Gloss and Bradlaw and Hillyard, or any one or two of them, that particular twist in the account would never have been included.'

'Why not?'

'Because it is one of those simple and rather pathetic circumstances that a murderer prefers to forget when thinking about his victim. He or his accomplice—and Gloss must have been one or the other if Gwill met his end this side of the front door—would only mention the sweet-eating if it were an essential part of his alibi or self-justification. And we haven't the slightest reason to suppose that it was either.'

Purbright patted Love's shoulder. 'Cheer up,' he said. 'What do you say we go next door and bully the poor widow-woman for a while?'

*   *   *

The widow-woman they found tweedy, business-like
and very self-possessed. She seemed, moreover, pleased
to see them—a bad sign in a witness, as Purbright
knew; for policemen, like illnesses, are best held at
bay by determined cheerfulness.

'How nice of you to come round,' she said. 'Yes, I
know you promised, but promises are made so often
in an attempt to be kind on the spur of the moment
and broken afterwards when sympathy has had time
to cool off.'

She led them into the large room facing Heston
Lane. It was tastefully and expensively furnished and
was far more attractive than its gloomy counterpart
at The Aspens.

'Do sit down,' said Mrs Carobleat. 'I've had not a
soul to talk to since the man came to read the meter
last week, and his conversation was limited, to put it
mildly. He has to save his breath to stoop into all
those little cupboards, I suppose.' She offered cigar-
rettes and lit one herself with a large table lighter.
'You'll have some tea, won't you?'

Not waiting for a reply, she darted to the door and
disappeared. They heard her giving brief instructions
at the rear of the house. Then, almost immediately,
she was back again. Whatever her age, Purbright reflected, she had a fitful energy and suppleness that be-
tokened a woman with plenty of money and no lack
of ideas of what to do with it. He realized that the
Joan Carobleat he had seen on two previous occasions had been an understatement of her proper self.
Six months ago, it was a newly bereaved wife with
whom he had dealt. Then, this past Tuesday in the
teashop, it was . . . well, what? A newly bereaved
mistress? Or just a woman wearied by a long rail
journey? In any case, here she was now, impressively
alert and sure of herself.

'It's only fair,' he told her, 'that you should know straight away that this is not a social call.'

She widened her eyes but continued to smile. 'Oh, come, inspector; all calls are social if those who make them have the grace to keep their real purpose to themselves until the kettle boils.'

Purbright decided to qualify for the compliment. He and his hostess shuttled small-talk for a while, watched politely by Love in the manner of a tennis spectator. Soon tea was brought on a large lacquered tray by a deferential, tight-lipped woman whom the policemen assumed to be a maid. They looked at her surreptitiously and with curiosity, for servants were not common in Flaxborough households. It was a bit like the pictures, Love told himself, adding the sour qualification that in real life the circumstance suggested ill-gotten gains.

Perhaps Purbright thought the same. He said: 'You seem to be managing fairly smoothly, Mrs Carobleat. On your own, that is. I admire you for it.'

'That is gallant of you, inspector. But you should reserve your admiration for my late husband's insurance company. I take no credit.'

'Financial independence doesn't always make widowhood easier to bear.'

'Doesn't it?' She explored a plate of biscuits and picked out a chocolate one.

'I should have thought the lack of companionship was the hardest part.'

'You are being very Godfrey Winney today, inspector. What are you after? A confession of my awful goings on with the gentleman next door?'

'I wouldn't dream of being so impertinent as to ask any such thing,' said Purbright. He turned to Love. 'You ask the lady, sergeant.'

Love's mouth fell open. Then he swallowed and grinned doubtfully. He was rescued by Joan Carob-

leat. She laughed and said: 'Never you mind, sergeant—Mr Purbright is just pulling our legs. Now,
then'—she faced Purbright again—'what is it you are
really after?'

'The murderer of the gentleman next door.'

'Yes, I suppose you are. . . .' Her voice was
suddenly grave. After a long pause she began stirring
her tea. As she watched a floating leaf whirl round
the rim, she said: 'You know I can't help, don't you? I
know nothing that could have the slightest bearing. I
wasn't even here.' She tried to capture the leaf on the
tip of her spoon, but it went by, revolving once more,
and sank.

'You saw a good deal of Gwill, didn't you?' Purbright asked.

'I seem to remember your putting that question before—in the teashop, wasn't it?'

'You said then that you had merely called occasionally as a neighbour. To cheer him up, or something.'

'That still expresses it adequately.'

'You were being facetious just now about some
"awful goings on".'

'I can be as facetious as I like about matters of
which you are now unlikely ever to be the wiser.'

'Mrs Poole might have given me a fairly clear idea
of your relationship.'

Mrs Carobleat smiled. 'A half-witted old servant?'

'You don't wish to confide in me any further, then?
I assure you I am the soul of tact and broad-minded-
ness. Come, now—you and Gwill were more than
pally neighbours, weren't you, Mrs Carobleat?'

She frowned, but not with annoyance. 'Look here,
inspector: suppose just for the hell of it I admitted
what Mrs Poole would call The Worst . . . just
what would be its bearing on your inquiries?'

'I might be a little nearer to discovering a motive

for what seems at the moment a singularly pointless crime.'

'Come, widows don't provide motives—except sometimes for other men's wives.'

'They occasionally have motives of their own. I don't suppose they are proof against being discarded, scorned, dishonoured—all that sort of thing, you know.'

She broke into a little clatter of laughter. Purbright, too, was smiling. But his eyes were alert.

'And how do you suggest this poor widow avenged her dishonour, inspector? When she wasn't even in the same town at the time?'

'You were in Hereford, you said?'

'Shropshire. The Lad's county, you know.'

'Ah, yes. You spent Monday night in a pub with a peculiar name. The Brink of Discovery.'

'I fancy its proprietor would prefer you to call it an inn. But at least you have the name right.'

'Was anyone else staying in this house while you were away? Your . . . the young woman who brought the tea?'

'Anna? Oh, no. She goes to some friends on a farm when I take a holiday. You were going to call her a maid, weren't you? She isn't quite that, actually. You could say companion if that doesn't make me sound terribly Bayswater. And old,' she added.

'You had no idea of what happened here until you returned from Shropshire and heard of Mr Gwill's death from me?'

'None whatever. It was hardly that the news would have reached me the same morning, even if anyone had thought I would wish to be told.'

'Hardly.' Purbright considered a moment. 'Did Mr Gwill have any . . . any presentiment of harm coming his way? Did he mention to you the possibility of his having an enemy?'

She pouted and shook her head.

'How did he get on with the men I presume to have been his friends—those who visited him regularly? Mr Gloss, for instance?'

'Gloss was his solicitor. He had quite a high opinion of him, I believe.'

'Dr Hillyard?'

'I really couldn't say.'

'Mr Bradlaw?'

'The undertaker, you mean? They were on good terms. They could do each other a certain amount of mutual good through the newspaper, of course. Advertising on one side, and help with lists of mourners and so forth on the other. It's a common enough arrangement, I believe.'

'Was there anyone apart from those three with whom Gwill was on intimate terms?'

'Not since my husband died. And always excepting his guilty association with me, of course.' Mrs Carobleat sipped her tea and eyed Purbright over the top of the cup.

After another quarter of an hour of being stolidly inquisitive to no perceptible effect, Purbright rose and said: 'You understand that I have no right at the moment to ask you this, but would you be willing just the same to let me have a look round your house?'

This, at any rate, seemed to find Mrs Carobleat unprepared. She looked at him doubtfully and said she couldn't quite see why, but he could if he really wanted to. He smiled apologetically and motioned her to lead the way.

The rest of the house proved to be as tidy, expensively furnished and well tended as the room they had left. Purbright and Love silently followed Mrs Carobleat, who only once turned in time to catch the inspector closely examining a power point.

He also showed interest in a small leather travelling case containing brushes and shaving equipment that lay on the dressing table of one of the only two bedrooms that showed signs of regular occupation.

'Those were Harold's,' she said expressionlessly. Purbright nodded and turned away.

CHAPTER TEN

On the morning following the publication day of the *Flaxborough Citizen*, an early telephone call was put through to the police station by George Lintz. Purbright had been in his office since the time he judged the first postal delivery would be made at the newspaper. He now hurried over to Market Street.

Lintz let him in and handed him fourteen letters addressed to the box numbers specified in the advertisements that had been inserted on his uncle's directions. An hour remained before members of the staff would begin to arrive. Purbright and Lintz settled into chairs in a small office on the first floor and waited for a kettle to boil on a gas ring in the fireplace.

The first envelope from which the flap curled back at the persuasion of steam and the somewhat self-conscious inspector contained a typewritten sheet and eight one-pound notes. The letter read:

Dear Sir,
   In response to your ad. I shall be pleased to call Tuesday at 7.45 p.m. to see goods as specified (Japanese antique newel, ebony) and enclose cash entitling me to first refusal of same. If inconvenient, kindly send card.

Yours faithfully,
H. L. Bird

* * *

The address at the top was 14, Burtley Avenue, Flaxborough.

Purbright read the letter through twice and handed it to Lintz. 'Bird . . . isn't that the agricultural machinery fellow?' Lintz looked at the address and nodded.

'What do you make of it?' Purbright had selected another letter from the pile and was carefully passing it to and fro across the gently steaming spout.

Lintz shrugged. 'He must be interested in antiques, I suppose. Not that I would have suspected Harry Bird of tastes in that direction. The money side of it is rather odd, isn't it?'

For answer, Purbright held up another bundle of notes that he had extracted from the second envelope. He counted them. There were eight. 'Standard rate, apparently,' he remarked and smoothed out the accompanying letter.

Dear Sir (it ran),
    Re your advert. in this week's issue, I wish to inspect goods on Thursday evening at 8 sharp. For preference Superior Antique Lampstand but would consider Jap Oak Antique Newel. Deposit herewith.

                              Yours truly,
                                N. Smith

The address was Derwentvale, Pawley Road, Flaxborough.

'Who's N. Smith?' Purbright asked, showing Lintz the letter.

'If he lives at that address, he's Councillor Herbert Smiles.'

'A doubly cautious buyer of antiques. Deals with

box numbers, and even then gives a false name. The cunning old councillor.' Purbright sounded far away. He was steaming another envelope with tender concentration as if it were a trout.

Once more he drew out notes—again eight. The letter followed the pattern of the first two, except that it contained a number of spelling mistakes. The signature, as far as Purbright could decipher, was R. Ocklom. The address was that of a shop in Harbour Road. Lintz said he thought it was a newsagent's and that it was an accommodation address. Purbright set to work on a fourth letter.

At the end of half an hour, the whole batch had been carefully disembowelled. Purbright took a large sheet of paper and began making a table of the various features of the correspondence. In the first column he set the name and address of each writer. In the second he put the date and time of the projected interview or appointment. The third received a description of the article that appeared to have been offered for sale.

Having completed this list, he restored the contents of all the envelopes, re-gummed the flaps and sealed them. Lintz took the bundle and returned the letters to the post box in the downstairs office.

A few minutes later, the first members of the newspaper staff came in. Avoiding them, Purbright and Lintz crossed the landing and went into the editor's own room. Somebody found the abandoned kettle, shook it and gratefully made some lumpy cocoa with its contents as a prelude to a dreary morning of preparing in advance the following week's 'What's On in Flaxborough.'

Purbright did not stay longer than was demanded by courtesy to one who now seemed less a suspect than a fellow conspirator. He enjoined Lintz, a little guiltily, to keep the oddities of Boxes CS.441/4 to himself and to place no obstacle in the way of the letters themselves being collected by anyone who might call for them. 'But ask your people to make sure and remember who it is,' he added.

Back at the police station, Sergeant Love wanted to know if the inspector thought it wise to have allowed Lintz to be a spectator of the letter opening.

'I don't see why not,' Purbright replied. 'After all, if he is involved, and if this antique business has a bearing on his uncle's death, it would be absurd for Lintz not to have used his position as editor to squash the whole thing. He had the opportunity to swipe Gwill's ledgers. He could have cooked up some simple explanation of the advertisements even after we had become suspicious. And there was nothing to stop him pretending that there had been no replies. Lintz might be fly, but I should be very surprised if he has a clue as to what old uncle was up to.'

'Yet even so, that wouldn't rule him out as the fellow we're looking for. The box reply racket may have nothing to do with the murder.'

Purbright smiled. 'In those letters that I've just steamed open there was money totalling a hundred and twelve pounds. When cash of that amount comes floating down into a murder case, you don't need to do much cherching of femmes or looking into family cupboards. Now then, let's see what we can make of all this.'

He spread out his tabulated digest of the box replies.

'Quite a social register,' Love remarked as he glanced down the first column. 'Are they genuine, do you think?'

'I'm sure they are. One or two are hiding behind false names, but they're pretty half-hearted deceptions. The addresses are real enough. Can you think why? That's the first point to consider.'

'How do you mean?'

'Well, the natural assumption is that the business, whatever it is, is shady. These respectable citizens must know it. Yet they pass cash over mostly genuine signatures and under entirely genuine addresses. That isn't quite what one would expect.'

Love tried hard. 'It suggests confidence, doesn't it?'

'Ah,' responded Purbright, 'you're right. These people are confident. We can be fairly sure, then,' he went on, 'that this means of communication, or doing business, or buying something—whatever it is—has been used by them over a long period. They trust it. Perhaps it's a game they enjoy for the sake of some little element of risk or thrill, as well. Another possibility, of course, is that the writer must identify himself properly, or substantially so, in case a reply or a cancellation needs to be sent. One letter actually said "if inconvenient, kindly send card". That was Harry Bird.'

'He makes reapers,' said Love, helpfully. The inspector considered this information for a moment but apparently found it irrelevant, as indeed it was. He waved his pencil over the second column of his table. 'Dates and times,' he murmured. 'What stands out here?'

Love read dutifully down the list, checking entries with the names and addresses beside them in the first column. 'All the times are in the evening,' he announced.

'They are, aren't they?'

'And on days during this next week.'

'Yes.'

'Well?' Love looked up.

'Nothing. I just wondered if a fresh young mind might spot something significant.'

The sergeant sniffed and glanced again through the

list of times. 'Seven to nine—they all fall between seven and nine.'

'So they do. Perhaps those are recognized antique viewing hours.'

The pencil hovered now over column three. 'What', asked Purbright, 'is an antique Japanese newel, for pity's sake?'

'A newel is a post. Something to do with a stair-case.'

Purbright said, 'Well, well,' and looked further down the inventory. 'Quite a number of them, aren't there? An old flourishing industry, do you think? In Japan, at any rate. . . . Ah, no, here is an Egyptian newel, inlaid dodecahedronic.'

'Bloody hell!' exclaimed Love.

Purbright reached down a dictionary from the shelf above his head and plunged after dodecahedronic. 'Something solid, with twelve equal sides,' he announced without enthusiasm. 'Where does that take us?'

'A robbery split twelve ways?' suggested Love recklessly. 'A fence's code, you know.'

'How ingenious. And Superior Antique Lampstand? What nefarious coup would you say that concealed?'

Love scowled and began to pick his teeth with a match. 'I know . . .' he said. 'Try other words with the same initials. S, A, L . . . smash and, smash and . . .'

'Languish? What about Swipe Auntie's Laundry?'

Both stared a little longer at the table. Then Love shrugged impatiently. 'There's only one thing to do. Pull in a couple of these characters and drag out of them what it's all about.'

Purbright pondered. He shook his head. 'No, not just yet. There may be a better way. Look—is there anyone in this lot who doesn't know you, who you can be sure wouldn't recognize you as a heavy-footed copper?'

Love looked over the names. 'There's Leadbitter here. He lives nearly opposite a sister of mine and I've seen him sometimes from her place when I've been there for tea. But I don't think he has any idea of who I am.'

'He's never been in court, has he?'

'Not to my knowledge. Certainly never when I've been there.'

'Good. Then tail him, Sid. His appointment is for the day after tomorrow at a quarter-past eight. You'd best make a day of it.'

'Follow him all day long?' Love, with memories of frozen feet in St Anne's Place, looked pained.

'Certainly. He's not likely to call and tell you when he's ready to go newel-viewing. If you try and pick him up in the evening, the odds are that you'll lose him. You'll have to keep him more or less in sight from when he leaves his house in the morning. Can that sister of yours put you up tomorrow night, do you think?'

'I imagine so.'

'That's all right, then. Has this fellow a car?'

'He ought to. He's the biggest meat wholesaler in Flaxborough.'

'In that case, Sid, we might stretch a point and let you borrow an o-fficial ve-hicle. Take the Hillman, and for heaven's sake don't scratch it or park it without lights or anything; the police are bastards in this town. Now let's see what our butcher friend is after in the antique line.' He traced Leadbitter on the list. 'Pewter Antique Tankard, indeed. And eight pounds. Always eight pounds. Why?'

'Probably as you said—a standard deposit.'

'Don't talk wet. No one puts deposits on things they haven't even seen. And these boys aren't after antiques anyway, Japanese or any other kind. From what I know of most of them, they couldn't tell a Queen Anne leg from the barmaid's elbow. Unless I'm mistaken, though, they have one thing in common.'

'Money,' said Love without hesitation.

'Exactly. And respectability. Wouldn't you say so?'

'Four of them are on the Council, if that counts for anything.'

'We'll allow that.'

'And eight . . . no nine, belong to the Country Club.'

'So does the Chief Constable. That should make them unimpeachable.'

Love opened his mouth, shut it, and then blurted: 'Look—I know it sounds corny, but what about blackmail?'

'Oh, Sid!' Purbright gave him an upward glance of sad remonstrance.

'Yes, but why not? These adverts could be a sort of reminder that another instalment of hush money is due. Look at the sort of people who reply—or pretend to be replying. They're all well known and well off, too. Gwill owned a newspaper. He could easily have found out things about them that they would be scared of seeing in print. We know that Gwill was careful to handle the adverts, and the box replies himself. It could be that the people paying him had been told to enclose a letter explaining the money in case an envelope went astray or got opened by one of the office staff by mistake.'

Purbright had listened attentively. 'Attractive,' he conceded. 'A neat idea. But it doesn't tie up with certain facts. In the first place, Gwill had been dead a couple of days, and known by the whole town to be dead, when these letters were sent off. Instead of posting their eight quidses, these people would have been celebrating the closing of the account.'

'Only if they knew who was blackmailing them,' said Love. 'We can't be sure that they did. In fact the whole beauty of the box reply system would have been the concealment of the blackmailer's identity.'

Purbright rubbed his cheek. 'That's perfectly true,' he said; then, with a frown, 'But why all this appointment nonsense? There could be no point in it once the money had passed over. Even as a blind for anyone who might open the letter by mistake it's unnecessarily elaborate.'

Dampened by this objection, Love decided against putting forward his final and most entrancing theory. Drugs, he calculated, was not the suggestion the inspector was waiting to hear.

CHAPTER ELEVEN

The account of the curious end of the proprietor of the *Flaxborough Citizen* that had been allowed to appear in his own publication was presented with none of the air of repressed delirium that had characterized earlier revelations in the national Press. But it was fulsome enough in its own way.

Once the *Citizen* had made it clear that the occasion was one it 'regretted to announce' and that the victim was the 'well-known public figure' who had enjoyed the privilege of being a 'principal in the town's leading printing and publishing concern', it treated his corpse pretty well like that of anyone else.

The inquest was reported in detail and, as if to compensate for the dullness of its formalities and its inconclusiveness, followed up by Inspector Purbright's intriguing request for information. This was enough to have most readers speculating happily on what had been going on and, indeed, on what was Up.

Purbright, for lack of anything better to do, took a copy of the paper along to the office of the Chief Constable. Mr Chubb had, as it turned out, read it already, and was now interested to know if some obliging witness had come forward to prove that the whole affair was just an unfortunate misunderstanding.

'You do see, don't you, my boy,' he explained in his

thin, cultured voice, dried up with calming important citizens and lecturing Flaxborough Historical Association on Bronze Age burial, 'that the sooner this business is cleared up the better? There is doubtless some quite simple explanation which eludes us. On reflection, I find it incredible that poor old Gwill would have been mixed up in anything, well, untoward.'

'I fully appreciate that, sir,' said Purbright. 'None of us cares for discredit to be hanging over the town.' Chubb nodded his approval to this sentiment. 'On the other hand, sir, it is my duty to advise you that all the inquiries we have made into the matter so far have all tended to strengthen the case for supposing Mr Gwill to have been murdered.'

The Chief Constable looked pained, then raised his brows in invitation to Purbright to elaborate this distasteful theme.

Purbright spread out a couple of sheets of paper on which he had jotted notes. Unhurriedly, he glanced over the main headings, read some of the paragraphs to himself, and then looked up to Chubb, who, on the inspector's entry, had levitated as usual while inviting his visitor to a chair and now leaned gracefully athwart a tall filing cabinet in one corner.

'It appears,' Purbright began, 'that contrary to our earlier supposition, Gwill was not alone in his house on the night of his death. Mr Gloss has since admitted that he was actually in the company of Mr Gwill until quite late. He has further alleged that Doctor Rupert Hillyard was with him also.

'His story was that while he and Doctor Hillyard were talking to Gwill, the telephone rang and Gwill answered it. In response to the call—and Mr Gloss says he couldn't gather who made it or what was said—Gwill is supposed to have hurried out of the house and not returned. If all this is true, the likelihood of a calculated attack on Gwill, or rather of some sort of trap laid for him, becomes very strong.'

Chubb shifted his position slightly to stare out of the window. 'Mr Gloss has acted rather foolishly in not coming forward at once with these facts. And I must say I'm surprised at Hillyard's reticence. He's said nothing to you, has he?'

'I haven't questioned him yet, sir.'

'All the same, the man surely must have realized something was wrong and that it was his duty to come along and give us what information he could. Of course'—Chubb turned to Purbright and smiled gently—'Hillyard's rather an odd chap in some ways. He's not always quite himself.' And with this indulgent interpretation, the Chief Constable's gaze went back to the sycamore against the further wall of the station courtyard.

Purbright continued. 'A witness has also been found who saw a van being driven out along Heston Lane late on Monday night and watched it return. Her description suggests that it was Mr Jonas Bradlaw's van. It seems very likely, in my opinion, that all three of them were there that night, and not just two.'

'Why should Mr Gloss not have mentioned Mr Bradlaw's presence, in that case?'

'I don't know, sir. One explanation could be that Mr Bradlaw and the doctor knew that they had been seen on their way to the house on foot but relied on no one having noticed Mr Bradlaw, who would have been pretty well concealed inside his van. It also happens that Mr Bradlaw went to some pains to establish an alibi for that time.'

'A false one, you mean?'

'It could very well be false.'

'Is there anyone else concerned, do you think?'

'I thought at first that the nephew was probably implicated.'

'The newspaper fellow?'

'Lintz, yes. But as time goes on he seems to slip further away as a possibility. For one thing, he was deliberately made part of Bradlaw's alibi, and nothing we've been able to find out suggests collusion between him and the other three. Still, we can't forget that he benefits materially from Gwill's death more obviously than anyone else.

'There is one other person,' went on Purbright, 'who I can't help feeling fits into the business in some way or other. Mrs Carobleat.'

Chubb gave him an inquiring glance. 'But she was miles away, surely?'

'So she says. I propose to have a word with the Shropshire people about that and perhaps take a trip over there myself. If you're agreeable, of course, sir.'

The Chief Constable looked doubtful. 'That's a bit out of the way, isn't it?'

'I shouldn't like to rely on another force making the sort of inquiries I have in mind, or I shouldn't hesitate to pass them on, sir. I've an idea that a close check on Mrs Carobleat's movements might be rewarding. It's almost certain that she was Gwill's mistress, and . . .'

'Oh, come; are you sure of that?' broke in Chubb, frowning.

'That's the consensus of opinion, I'm afraid, sir.'

'You don't suggest the woman might have had a hand in the fellow's murder?'

'I shall be in a better position to say when we know what she was doing at the operative time, sir. And before, of course. The fact that she was away at all may have significance.'

Chubb sighed. 'These affairs are damnably unpleasant. All this questioning and poking into other

people's business. I don't know how you bring yourself to do it, Purbright, I don't, really. The only other
murder in Flaxborough I can remember was quite
different. It was the shooting of old Mrs Donovan by
Hargreaves, the pet-shop man. He was the perfect
gentleman, poor Hargreaves. Came along here
straight away afterwards and stood waiting at the
counter downstairs until someone had time to attend
to him. Then he handed over the revolver—he'd put
it in a clean paper bag, I remember—and put
eightpence in the Boot and Shoe Fund box, then
confessed as nicely as you like. He used to keep that
shop a perfect picture.'

Purbright bore with this reminiscence and then
told Chubb about his arrangements for investigating
the matter of the advertisements in the *Citizen*.

The Chief Constable listened. 'My, but you're
being kept busy,' he said. 'It's amazing, isn't it, how
many odd little things go on under the surface of a
place like this?'

'Yes, isn't it, sir,' agreed Purbright. 'Takes all sorts
to make a world.' Not for the first time, he was visited
with the suspicion that Chubb had donned the uniform of head of the Borough police force in a moment of municipal confusion when someone had
overlooked the fact that he was really a candidate for
the curatorship of the Fish Street Museum.

'When do you think we can expect an arrest, my
boy?' asked Chubb. 'Or would that,' he added in
bloodless parody of jocularity, 'be telling?'

Purbright clenched his teeth.

Mr P. F. F. Smith, manager of the Flaxborough
branch of the Eastern Provinces and Bartonshire Con-
solidated Bank, rose and greeted his visitor with almost explosive affability. He had made sure, when
the appointment was being fixed, that none of the

bank's much advertised services and favours would be invoked.

'Grand day,' beamed Mr. Smith, motioning Purbright to The Customer's chair.

'Well, it's cold and rather foggy outside, actually,' Purbright corrected him.

'Yes, how miserable,' agreed Mr Smith. 'Seasonable for the time of year, though.' He grinned over the gleaming nakedness of his desk top, on the very edge of which his aseptically manicured fingers beat a refined tattoo.

'We should be glad to have your help, sir . . .'

Mr Smith inclined his head and continued to register delight. 'Anything we can do, we shall be only too pleased.'

'. . . in a somewhat delicate matter,' Purbright added, and the tiniest flake of frost settled upon Mr Smith's manner.

'You will have heard of the death last Monday night of Mr Marcus Gwill?'

'Indeed, yes. A shocking affair. A gentleman and a most charming man.'

'You found him so, sir?'

'Oh, yes.' A slight pause. 'Within the limits of our professional relationship, of course. What was, er, your impression, inspector?'

'If I had formed one, it would scarcely be relevant to my present inquiries, sir.'

'Quite so.' Mr Smith nodded and gave the first of the tiny, flicked glances at the clock above Purbright's head that were to accompany his every second remark throughout the interview.

'But the general impression conveyed to me by others is that Mr Gwill was not outstandingly easy to get along with.'

'I can quite understand that, inspector, now that you mention it. He was reserved, you know, and perhaps just the least bit forbidding. Charm was not his strong suit.'

'What I have to ask you, Mr Smith, is not so much concerned with the gentleman's character as with his cash. He dealt predominantly with this bank, I understand.'

'I see no harm in confirming that he did have a private account with us.' Mr Smith's eye was now more watchful within its smiling socket.

'Small or large?'

'Of late, quite substantial. And it was about to become much more substantial, as you no doubt know already.'

'I don't, as it happens, sir. I wonder if you'd care to tell me about that?'

'Ah . . .' Mr Smith had realized his indiscretion. 'I think perhaps you should not press me in these somewhat confidential matters, inspector. A client's affairs are with us—what shall I say?—like the secrets of the confessional.'

'But not, surely, after he's been murdered, Mr Smith?'

'Murdered?' The manager succeeded in looking as if Purbright had suddenly asked for an overdraft.

'Oh, yes. So now he's my client as well, in a sense.'

'I see. . . . But how dreadful.'

'This is news to you?'

'But decidedly. I had no idea.'

'Except for rumours, perhaps?'

Mr Smith shrugged delicately. 'We make it our business not to pay too much attention to rumour, inspector. The bank likes to be absolutely sure of everything.'

'So do the police, sir. That is why I have presumed to trespass upon your time.'

Mr Smith nodded sagaciously and joined his fingertips. 'Please ask me anything you like, inspector. It is

the duty of us all to co-operate in the solution of
crime, especially'—his smile returned and resumed its
seat, as it were, upon the smooth cushions of his
face—'especially when the victim is a person of integ-
rity.'

'And recently augmented substance,' Purbright put
in, suggestively.

'Ah, yes. I was about to elaborate on that theme,
was I not? Well, the addition to Mr Gwill's fortunes,
such as they were, was to have been brought about
under the terms of the will, of course.'

'The will?'

'Yes. The late Councillor Carobleat's bequest. A
matter of'—Mr Smith rolled his eyes upward for a moment—'oh, some eighteen thousand pounds.'

Purbright frowned. 'But surely he left a widow?'

'Ah, the widow. Yes.' Mr Smith picked an invisible
thread from his cuff. 'A peculiar circumstance, that.
But the will was quite explicitly in Mr Gwill's favour—and in that of certain other beneficiaries. Mrs
Carobleat has not suffered as much as you might
think, however.'

'Insurance?'

'Er, so I am led to understand. A substantial sum.
Then there was the house, and so forth. She is well
provided for.'

'That was my impression,' said Purbright. 'Even so,
it isn't customary to will away all one's money over a
wife's head, so to speak.'

'Quite so. It came as a surprise to me, I admit. I
had expected Carobleat to be found to have died in-
testate, as a matter of fact. It was only a short time
before his illness that the question of wills cropped
up in conversation between us. He gave me to understand that he had taken no steps in that direction.
Naturally, I urged upon him the desirability of making proper provision, but he gave no sign of taking

me seriously. Yet the will must already have been in existence at that very time, although it didn't actually come to light for some little while after his death.'

'And how was that?'

'I'm not sure that I ought to tell you, inspector.' Mr Smith regarded his finger-ends as though his professional conscience pulsed there, just below the skin that had flicked back without temptation the corners of untold thousands of banknotes. 'You might think that someone had been a little remiss, although I'm sure it was simply a matter of a slight lapse in office routine. Not all firms are run as punctilliously as banks, you know.'

'The will was mislaid?'

Mr Smith leaned forward. 'Strictly between ourselves,' he said, 'it was. Gloss explained afterwards how it had happened. Well, of course, he had to be absolutely frank about it, because of the possibility of its being challenged by the widow. She didn't, as it happens, but never mind.'

He remained silent for some time.

'Well?' Purbright prompted.

'Well what?' countered Mr Smith.

'The will,' said Purbright. 'You were saying how it came to be mislaid.'

'Ah . . . I can't say that I remember precisely. It was quite a silly, simple sort of reason—put in the wrong deed box, or something like that. But it came to light eventually. The money hasn't been turned over yet, by the way. Executing a will takes quite a while. But it was definitely on the turn, if you follow me. How galling it must be to die just too soon to enjoy a legacy that you know is practically in your hand—in your account, rather.' Mr Smith shook his head and closed his eyes in brief mourning for Mr Gwill's ravished opportunities.

'Gwill's account was separate, I suppose, from the finances of his newspaper company?'

'Oh, yes, naturally.'

'And would you say that his income as shown by the private account was consistent with the earnings he received from the company?'

Mr Smith looked sharply at the inspector. 'No,' he replied simply, 'I should not.'

'He was receiving money from another source?'

'Almost certainly he was. Not that it was any concern of mine, of course, but these little impressions register, you know, in spite of ourselves.'

'Yes, don't they. Incidentally, have you retained any impression of what that source was, sir?'

'None whatever.'

'Because the money was deposited in cash?'

Mr Smith flexed his facial muscles in a smile. 'There are, as they say, no flies on you, inspector.'

Purbright acknowledged the compliment with a grunt. He had concluded by now that Mr Smith was not merely fly-proof but probably impervious to attack and courtship alike by all creatures whatsoever.

'You have been most helpful, sir,' he said, rising.

The manager, though not appearing to move, was suddenly transposed to the door of his office, which he flung open while extending his free hand in an ushering gesture of brotherly dismissal. 'Not at all, inspector. Delighted.' In the instant before turning back to his desk, he darted a glance at the three counter clerks and gave an inward click of satisfaction on noting that the entire trio was immersed in work.

CHAPTER TWELVE

If Alderman Leadbitter had been less preoccupied with wholesale meat deals, bottles of pale ale, and a certain matter that had filled him with secret excitement since his rising that morning shortly before eight o'clock, he could not have failed to be conscious of a radiant pink orb that had hung in the background all that day. As it was, Sergeant Love's face had been a mere blurred iridescence amongst the other unnoticed details of his surroundings.

Which was fortunate, for the sergeant was not adept at self-effacing observation. When he wished to see without being seen, he adopted an air of nonchalance so extravagant that people followed him in expectation of his throwing handfuls of pound notes in the air.

He had got up much earlier than his quarry, and by six o'clock was posted, already shaved, washed and hastily fed, behind his sister's lace curtains, staring at the dark shape opposite, within which still slumbered the alderman and his family. It was not until nearly four hours later that signs of activity prompted him to go out into the cold and pretend to tinker under the bonnet of the police car, which he had left ready to drive out of the gate.

Alderman Leadbitter's car appeared at half-past ten and was driven slowly by its owner to his office in Pipeclay Lane, near the slaughterhouses. After some twenty minutes, he walked out of the office and passed Love, seated in his car which he had parked very wrongfully opposite a cattle unloading bay.

The sergeant followed him on foot and was led to the Golden Keys Hotel. There, he drank slowly and without much enjoyment two half pints of mild while the alderman swallowed six glasses of bottled beer at the opposite end of the long saloon bar in the company of several other civic luminaries before returning to his counting house at nearly one o'clock.

Leadbitter went home for his lunch, so Love's sister served her brother with a meal on the bamboo table in the front room. He ate speedily and with a constant eye on the opposite door, so that when he resumed the trail he was suffering the handicap of hiccups.

The afternoon proved no more eventful than the morning. By the time the alderman's car drew up at his home for the second time that day, Love was wondering why he had wasted so many hours in dull and fruitless surveillance instead of relying on Leadbitter being a man of regular and proper habits that included taking five-o'clock tea in the bosom of his family.

Later still, when it was quite dark and he sat in the cold car, drawing what comfort he could from a cigarette, he was gradually overtaken by a sense of anticlimax.

Suppose the alderman and the other people who had replied to the advertisements really were buyers of odd and ends? The things might be genuine and a seemingly eccentric way of disposing of them might be the method of doing business chosen by some exclusive private dealer. Yet surely that standardized eight pounds deposit was too fantastic a condition of sale to be acceptable even to someone mad enough to want a—what was it again?—a Japanese newel post.

A tankard it was for Leadbitter. A pewter antique tankard, he'd said.

Love repeated the phrase to himself several times. Then he realized why it had struck him as odd from the first. The order of words was queer.

Any normal person surely would have written antique pewter tankard. Or, in catalogue and army style, Tankard, antique pewter. But never pewter antique tankard. Why had the words been put in that sequence?

Again Love allowed his fancy to stray outside the local probabilities. He considered codes. Pewter . . . Antique . . . Tankard . . . It couldn't be a letter by letter code. That kind did not form actual words. In any case, it would be expecting far too much of people like Flaxborough's successful business men to grasp anything so complicated.

Could each word have some prearranged significance, then? That was more probably the explanation. If it were, there was no hope of finding the meaning of the advertisements by ordinary systems of de-coding—even if he knew what these were, which he didn't, except for a vague idea that the most frequently recurring symbol would represent E, and what was the use of a string of E's, anyway?

Right, then, ruminated Love, each of the three words meant something quite different. Pewter?—cocaine, perhaps. Antique? The quantity, say. And tankard? There was only one factor left for that to represent—the price asked. 'Please have ready for me at 8:15 p.m. two pounds of your best cocaine at . . . at . . . fifteen and six an ounce.' How cold and cramped he was growing. Damn Purbright and Leadbitter and tankards and codes and . . . He sat up and peered through the windscreen. At last, the alderman's door was opening.

Five minutes later, Love drew up at a discreet dis-

tance from Leadbitter's car in the forecourt of the
Golden Keys. Leadbitter was not in search of the
saloon company this time. He hurried into a small
room on the other side of the corridor.

Love lingered near the entrance. It was not yet
eight o'clock, and although he felt confident that
Leadbitter had not noticed his pursuit up to now, he
did not want to commit himself to an encounter at
close quarters until the last possible moment. Regret-
fully he watched a waitress carry what appeared to be
a whisky into the room Leadbitter had entered, then
he retraced his steps to the car.

To the policeman's considerable relief, Leadbitter
soon reappeared. Instead of getting into the car
again, however, he set off along Hooper Rise and
turned right into Spoongate. Love followed, keeping
to the opposite pavement. For the first time that day,
the alderman appeared slightly apprehensive. He
even glanced back on several occasions, but saw nothing to make him reduce his pace.

Suddenly, Love realized that the other was no longer in front. He halted, momentarily panic-stricken,
and stared over the road at the point where Leadbitter had vanished.

Dark, pillared doorways faced him, all much alike
in the gloom. There was no sound but that of a wireless on one of the upper floors. He remained motionless, straining eye and ear.

Then from one of the porches came a shaft of yellow light. Love mentally fixed its position and was already walking diagonally across the road towards it
when it narrowed to a slit and was eclipsed altogether. A gentle thud and the reappearance of the
light, widening and narrowing by turn, told Love
that the door which almost certainly had admitted
Leadbitter had been left on the latch and was swinging in the light wind.

Love walked cautiously up the four steps that led to the doorway. On one side he saw the gleam of metal. It was a name plate. He stopped and tried to read it, but the nearest street lamp was thirty yards away. Just as he was fumbling for matches, the door swung back and a woman stepped out into the porch. Love straightened up guiltily and looked at her. 'It's all right,' she said. 'They've started.' 'Oh,' said Love, 'thank you.' The woman wished him good night and descended the steps. Now that the door was wide open, the name on the plate was perfectly clear. It was R. Hillyard, M.D.

The panelled hallway into which Love stepped, closing the door gently behind him, had once been warmly luxurious, but the constant passage of patients had given it a shabby, polish-starved look. The elegance of its proportions still made immediate impression, however, and Love glanced admiringly at the slim-banistered staircase and the lofty window at its head. The house was a much larger one than the narrow façade suggested.

The nearest door on the right was ajar. Love heard from the room beyond an occasional sniff, a cough or two and an assortment of shuffles and creaks. It was without doubt the doctor's waiting-room. He entered, sat down as near the door as he could manage, and after the preliminary devotions usual in such places—brief contemplation of his knees and a slow search round the walls for a non-existent clock—he surreptitiously looked over the eight or nine people present.

They were a typical surgery selection. A young woman who met his glance with a resentful stare, signifying that she held the male species malignantly responsible for all abdominal irregularities whatsoever. A sunken-cheeked man with scrubby grey hair and an internal whistle. A middle-aged matron with Bad Leg.

A nervous young man who had been reading too many truss advertisements.

But of Alderman Leadbitter there was no sign. Wherever pewter antique tankards were being displayed that evening, it was not in the company of these unexceptional specimens of ailing humanity.

Love pondered what he should do next. Obviously he would be wasting his time and ruining a whole day's tedious work by staying where he was.

He got up and went out into the hallway, watched with mournful contempt by the waiting patients. The rest of the house was silent. It might, he guessed, be largely unoccupied. There were five other doors on this floor and he walked quickly from one to another. At each he listened briefly. Behind only one was there a sound. It was a mumbled conversation between a woman and a man with a Scots accent. Love decided that this must be Hillyard's consulting room. He heard nothing of the boomingly hearty voice of Alderman Leadbitter.

On tiptoe he climbed rapidly to the first turn of the staircase, paused to listen again, then ascended more slowly to the floor above.

Fixed to the wall opposite the head of the stairs was a small green baize notice board, to which a typed sheet was pinned.

The paper bore the day's date and was marked off into three columns.

In the first was what seemed to be a series of times, varying between 7:30 and 8:30. The second column contained numbers—either 1, 2, 3 or 4. In the third were sets of initials.

At the head of the sheet were the words 'Treatment Schedule.'

Love, wary by now of code theories, contented himself with rapidly jotting a copy of the table into his notebook. He had barely finished when a door shut loudly somewhere on his left. He darted instinctively in the opposite direction and drew himself into the deeply shadowed corner of the landing farthest from the staircase wall.

A man emerged from an opening in the wall about ten feet beyond the notice board. He was wearing an overcoat and carried a hat. At the top of the stairs he halted and stood looking down into the hall for several seconds. Then he began to descend. A minute later Love heard the gentle thud of the front door.

This was interesting. The man was Herbert Stamper, who farmed on the west side of Flaxborough Fen: a prosperous and venal gentleman, much troubled by the stubborn survival of an ailing and intolerant wife. Love recalled that his name had appeared on Purbright's list of antique fanciers.

From below came the noise of voices. Love peered cautiously over the rail and saw a woman coming out of what he had assumed to be the surgery door. Some sort of cheery farewell was being wished her from within the room. As finally she turned and crossed the hall, a buzzer sounded and the chesty man, with wheeze at full cock, slouched from the waiting-room to the doctor's door.

Love turned back and sought the point at which Mr Stamper had made his appearance. It proved to be the entrance to a corridor that ran at right angles to the landing wall. An arrowed card, bearing the direction 'Treatment cubicles (Male Patients)', hung from a nail. Four doors, at intervals of several feet, were set along the left wall of this passage. The end appeared to be blank.

Exploring further along the landing, Love discovered another corridor, running parallel to the first. In this case, however, its four doors were on the right. The card at the corner announced 'Treatment cubicles (Female Patients)'. Love turned back and re-en-

tered the male corridor, feeling that at this stage the
proprieties ought to be observed.

He put his ear to the door marked '1'. There was
silence inside. Slowly he turned the handle and
pressed against the panels. The door would not move.
Then he pulled and found the door had been made
to open outwards. The space within was little bigger
than a cupboard. It was fitted with a mirror and
clothing hooks and seemed intended to serve as a
small dressing-room. There was another door immediately opposite. Love tried it, but it had been locked
or bolted from the other side. No sound came from
whatever lay beyond.

Love stood wondering how much longer he would
be able to poke his way around the private house of a
doctor against whom he had no evidence or even
what a magistrate would deem reasonable suspicion
of criminal activity, and how he would explain his
presence there if challenged. Both questions defeated
him, so he put them resolutely from his mind and
puzzled instead over a noise that reached him faintly
from a direction he could not fix.

He went back into the corridor and tried the door
numbered '2'. As he opened it, the sound he wanted
to identify grew louder. He listened. There was no
doubt about it. Leadbitter had been run to earth.

The noises that came through the inner door of the
closet were those of the alderman repressing his normal boom to a confidential growl, interspersed with
asinine chuckles. The general effect was curious. Love
thought it suggested mild delirium under anaesthetic.

Was Leadbitter undergoing a minor operation of
some kind? It was possible. The clothing he had been
wearing during the day was hung untidily on the
hooks at the side of the cupboard-like compartment
and tossed on the narrow bench below them. Love

checked them over. Only socks and shirt appeared to be missing.

He pressed his ear to the inner door. The alderman's noises were now faint and intermittent. A sigh . . . a groan . . . a contented gasp. . . . The anaesthetic must have taken effect. Very gently, Love tried the door. It would not yield.

As he stood looking at it, he heard footsteps approaching fairly rapidly along the corridor. He turned to close the cubicle door but realized that this would entail reaching out of his present comparatively secure shelter.

Before he could make up his mind what to do, a shadow fell across the entrance. He did his best to defend his position by staring boldly straight into the face of the large man who now peered in at him.

Surprisingly enough, the new arrival did no more than pause, deliver a friendly wink, and pass on along the corridor. A door opened and closed—Love judged it to be the last in the row—and there was silence once more. Not even an aldermanic grunt broke the stillness.

Going out into the corridor again, Love reflected on the stranger's amiability. He supposed the wink to have been a natural gesture for one patient to make to another. The *camaraderie* of hospitals, he heard, was a jolly business, maintained by fellow sufferers to minimize their apprehension of knives, needles and other surgical terrors.

He eased open the door of the third cubicle. There was no clothing in this one. Automatically, he tried the farther door. To his surprise, it moved freely, and he was just in time to tighten his grip on the handle to prevent the door swinging open away from him. With his free hand he pulled the outer door closed at his back and stood for some seconds in the resultant darkness before beginning to edge his way slowly into the space ahead.

The room, if that was what it was, was comfortably warm, but absolutely dark. Love took tiny, silent steps forward, feeling tensely for obstacles with feet and outstretched hands. It was not his sense of touch, though, but his ears that warned him to pause.

Somewhere in front of him, quite near, was being made a soft rhythmical sound. It was, he thought, a sort of gentle brushing, regular and mechanical. Brushing—or dragging, perhaps. As he listened, an earlier speculation returned to mind and was instantly mated to the new problem. Of course—anaesthesia. It was a pump or respirator of some kind that he now could hear. He recalled an operation scene in a film, where bladders softly inflated and deflated as the surgeons bent over their task.

But why no lights?

Slowly and with infinite caution, Love slithered first one foot, then the other, over the carpet. Carpet? He frowned. Hospitals never had carpets. But that wasn't to say private clinics did not. Never mind, he was nearing whatever was making the soft exhalations. He felt in his overcoat pocket for the torch he carried. The time had come for a showdown, whatever the consequences. He could always plead lost directions. He levelled the torch and slid his thumb to its button. . . .

For years afterwards, Love was to question his ridiculous, his lunatic failure to identify the simple sound that had guided him across the floor that night. As the light beam leaped alarmingly ahead, Love jumped as if he held a recoiling cannon in his hand.

From a couch five feet distant was rearing up in fright and indignation the lady whose measured breathing in a contemplative doze he had so fantastically misinterpreted.

In the fraction of time before he turned and rushed with mumbled apologies in the direction whence he had come, the policeman noticed two things.

One was the identity of the outraged female.

The second was the lady's bizarre choice of costume: a heavy glass necklace and a pair of stockings, one slightly laddered.

It was not until later that a third, no less curious, circumstance registered. He recalled that she had flung after his retreating figure the epithet 'bloody old devil!', together with several kinds of threats of what would happen if he 'tried a trick like that again'.

What did she mean by 'old', Love asked himself with some annoyance as he tramped back to where he had left the car.

CHAPTER THIRTEEN

Purbright was still in his office when Love drove the car into the police garage and walked past the night sergeant, who had begun his mysterious routine of entering things laboriously in books and juggling with plugs and cords on the switchboard.

The inspector listened attentively to the story of the shadowing of Alderman Leadbitter. He drew towards him a pad of paper, an ashtray and a cup half-full of cold, grey coffee.

'Now, Sid; let's have that list you copied from the board on the landing.'

At Love's direction, he marked out three columns and began filling them with the numbers and letters in the sergeant's notebook. Then he pulled from a file the table he had compiled earlier of names, specifications and times contained in the answers to the advertisements in the *Citizen*.

'By the way,' said Love, 'did you find who collected those box replies?'

Purbright nodded. 'A young fellow from Gloss's office. Lintz told me. I cornered the lad this afternoon, as a matter of fact, and he said his boss had sent him with the ticket—the counterfoil that's issued when anyone places an advert—to pick up any letters under that number.'

'That would leave Gloss with something to explain, then.'

'He made no bones about it. He said the ticket had been amongst Gwill's papers that he, as his solicitor, had been sorting out, and that he thought he'd better see if there was anything urgent about the business.'

'Had he the letters there?'

'Oh, yes. All opened. He was most obliging. Showed them to me and asked me what I thought they could mean. The money was there, too.'

'Could he explain that?'

Purbright sighed. 'My dear Sid, you should know by now that we've got everything out of that gentleman that he'll part with until we can use the rack.'

He put the two lists side by side and began comparing them. His pencil point wavered from one column to another, pounced on a number or a set of initials, then moved beneath a name, an address, a date. Twenty minutes went by. Love got up, looked disconsolately out of the uncurtained window at the blackness bloomed with a dim reflection of the room's lamp-light upon rags of mist, and walked to the door. 'I'll see if Charlie can fix up a mug of something,' he said, and departed.

Purbright's manner of scrutinizing the pages before him became gradually more alert. Several details were now underlined. He passed his tongue over his dry upper lip and reached for the coffee cup. Absentmindedly he sipped its chilled, forbidding residue.

When Love came back with two steaming mugs, he motioned him to his side and pointed to one of the entries he had marked.

'This is interesting. Edward Leadbitter, you notice, wrote asking to see an antique pewter tankard . . .'

'A pewter antique tankard.'

'Eh? All right, then, a pewter antique tankard; and he specified eight-fifteen this evening. Now then'—Purbright moved his pencil over to the second sheet—'here's the entry on that upstairs board of Hillyard's. First of all, the time. Eight-fifteen. That checks. Next, the figure two. You said it was the second cubicle from which you heard his voice. Now in the last column on the notice board are these five initials: E.L.P.A.T.'

Love scratched his chin.

'Edward . . .' Purbright prompted.

'Edward Leadbitter . . . Pewter . . . Of course, it's that bloody tankard again.'

'Exactly.'

'But I still can't see any sense in it,' protested Love. 'The place hadn't an antique in sight. No pewter, no furniture, nothing like that at all. It was like a clinic or part of a hospital, except that it was more comfortable. It was certainly no antique that jumped up at me when I switched the torch on.' Love looked more gleeful than dismayed at the memory of the moment of revelation before his flight.

'Never mind the Venusberg aspect. Who was the fellow you said you saw on the landing?'

'Stamper. Bert Stamper.'

'The farmer?'

'That's the one, yes.'

Purbright looked down the names on his letter digest. 'Here we are—he just put initials to his reply. H.S. And over here'—he waved his pencil over to the 'Treatment Schedule'—'they appear against seven-thirty and cubicle three.'

'Three was the cubicle where I found the door unlocked.'

'And looked at what the policeman saw.'

Love blushed happily.

'You say you know the girl?'

'Professionally, yes. Mrs Shooter—Margaret Shooter, I believe it was. I was beat-bashing in those days and she was listed with a few others for entertaining sailors in the place in Broad Street.'

'Over by the harbour?'

'Yes. There used to be more knocking shops than telegraph poles down there at one time. That was before Holy Harry blew out all the red lamps and set the girls to sew surplices.'

Purbright looked pained. 'Don't come that hell's kitchen stuff to me, Sid. You know perfectly well that the Flaxborough brand of vice was never anything but shabby amateurism. The house you're talking about closed down weeks before we could get any real evidence. By Holy Harry, I suppose you mean the late and questionable Mr Carobleat?'

'That's the boy.'

'I'd never heard the soul-saving line before. What we suspected was that he got hold of a list of the ladies we were interested in when he was chairman of the Watch Committee and went round tipping them off.'

'They stopped operating, anyway,' said Love defensively.

'So far as we could prove, they did. But don't delude yourself that they took to good works. However'—Purbright looked at his watch—'that's neither here nor there. Let's finish with Stamper, the honest hayseed.'

He sipped from the mug Love had brought in and found his place again in the letters summary. 'It was the heavy stuff he was after, apparently. A mahogany and beech sideboard, of all things. Did you happen to trip over any sideboards in your flight from Mrs Shooter?'

Love looked at the second sheet. 'There you are.' He pointed to a group of initials, six this time. 'That's clear enough—Herbert Stamper, Mahogany And Beech Sideboard.' He ran his fingers through his hair. 'Maybe the place is a private asylum.'

Purbright leaned back in his chair and stared into

space. 'You say you don't know the big man who looked in at you while you were in Leadbitter's cubicle. And yet he winked at you?'

'Oh, yes. Quite friendly, he seemed.'

'A wink,' Purbright went on, talking half to himself, 'suggests sharing a joke, a lark, as you might say. Something private and perhaps risky or pleasantly scandalous. But not'—he joined his fingers—'desperately conspiratorial. No murders or burglaries. And no drugs, I fancy: that's commonly a gloomy or else a hysterical business. Could that wink, though, have been one purely of medical commiseration between fellow candidates for boil lancing or colonic irrigation?'

'What's that?' asked Love.

'Enemas.'

'He didn't look as if there was anything wrong with him. And I'm sure he couldn't have thought I wanted an enema.'

Purbright glanced at him briefly and again addressed the ceiling. 'No, I'm sure he couldn't. So there must be some other reason for the recognition of one man of the world by another.' Love lifted one eyebrow, but said nothing.

'These cubicle things,' said Purbright. 'Would you say they'd been there long? Were they an original part of the house?'

'I don't think so. They looked like conversions. Not brand new, but recent.'

'Solid?'

'Well . . .' Love considered. 'I don't know much about building, but they looked a pretty sound job of carpentry. Sort of semi-permanent.'

'You didn't go down the second corridor?'

'No, there was a sign up . . .'

'Ah, yes, I'd forgotten.' Purbright was silent. Then

he looked again at his watch and yawned. 'We do see life, don't we?' He began tidying up his desk.

Before Love could ask what he was supposed to deduce from the evening's events, he heard footsteps approaching from the main office. Purbright listened. 'The Chief Constable,' he said, 'is upon us.'

Mr Chubb knocked punctiliously before entering. He wore a grey overcoat of remarkable rigidity and carried a bowler hat and what he himself would have termed a gamp. He looked as if he might have been attending a public meeting of the better, quieter sort; of the Friends of Flaxborough Cathedral, say.

'Ah, Purbright,' he said, with 'Evening, sergeant' in kindly parenthesis, 'I've just come from having a word or two with the Coroner. No, sit down, sit down.' He propped himself against a cupboard in his customary attitude of elegant detachment and gave the impression of being ready to hear petitioners. After some seconds he said: 'He wants to get this Gwill business cleared up, you know. Amblesby's rather old for adjournments. He can't always remember what he's adjourned or why.' Mr Chubb permitted himself a weak smile, then extinguished it and added: 'A perfectly sound old fellow, of course.'

'Oh, yes,' Purbright agreed, with a shade of querulousness.

'You're still confident poor Gwill was deliberately, er . . .'

'Quite, sir.'

'Mmm . . .' Mr Chubb regarded his yellow knitted gloves. 'Anything turned up since last we talked about it?'

Purbright salvaged his file from the drawer into which he had pushed it a few moments before and turned over a few pages of notes. 'I had quite an interesting conversation with Mr Smith, of the Eastern Provinces,' he announced.

'Percy Smith. Oh, yes; I know him very well. Extremely sound on coarse fishing. Not terribly forthcoming, though, as a rule.'

'No, sir,' Purbright agreed drily. 'But he did confide that Gwill was a beneficiary under the will of the late Mr Harold Carobleat—they were next door neighbours, if you remember, sir—in spite of the widow having been left nothing. And he also admitted that Gill received and deposited sums of money in cash that appeared to have had nothing to do with his newspaper business.'

'Goodness me,' said the Chief Constable, tonelessly. He looked at Love, then back to Purbright. 'Do you suppose that what Smith told you—the money side of it, one might say—had anything to do with the poor fellow coming to a sticky end? Of course,' he added hastily, 'that will business sounds absolutely incredible. It does, really.'

Purbright replied that it was beginning to appear, in his opinion, that Gwill's mysterious source of income might have had a great deal to do with his death and, further, that the arranging and accomplishment of his murder could no longer be assumed to have been the work of a specific individual.

'You think several people might have been in it?'

'Three, sir. Probably four. Perhaps even five.'

'Not Flaxborough people, surely?' There was a note of pleading in Mr Chubb's voice.

'Those I have in mind are no strangers to the town, sir.'

The Chief Constable compressed his thin mouth, walked slowly across to Purbright's desk and actually drew up a chair for himself. Then he sighed and said: 'You'd better give me the names, my boy. Might as well know where we are. You could be wrong, of course.'

'Oh, certainly,' Purbright agreed. 'I hope I am. But

if it turns out that only one person did it, after all, it will be rather nice to feel that four citizens have been restored, as you might say.'

He went on, briskly: 'As a matter of fact, you have the names already. I ran over them when I saw you after the inquest opening. They are all the obvious ones, of course, but I see no reason for discarding them on that account. Gloss presents an interesting study. He is a man whom professional training should have taught to leave no part of his dealings with the dead man capable of being interpreted unfavourably. Yet scarcely is the crime discovered before he is round to see you, sir, with hints of secret knowledge and personal danger. He admits to me his presence in Gwill's house on the night of the murder. He is surprisingly frank about certain financial aspects of his client's affairs. He gives all sorts of unexpected replies to questions. In short, he asks so persistently to be suspected that we can be quite sure he is trying to lead us along a blank alley, at the end of which he will have no difficulty in refuting and specific charge we might feel constrained to level against him.'

Love looked on in undisguised admiration of Purbright's dialetic. Then he glanced to see how Mr Chubb was taking it.

The Chief Constable roused himself to ask: 'But what hard evidence have you to support all this? It sounds—if you'll forgive me saying so—just a fraction theoretical. I must admit,' he added almost with warmth, 'that I never suspected you of applying such . . . such a wealth of psychology, as you might say. I'd always thought traffic was your forte. But it's the unexpected that really puts us all to the test. Pity, in one sense, that we're rather badly off for crime round here. Nastiness is as much as most of them can rise to.'

'Then there is Doctor Hillyard,' Purbright went on,

keeping to his own track. 'Hillyard was Gwill's doctor and on fairly close social terms with him. He also was present at his home on the night of the murder. It may or may not be significant that Hillyard was the doctor in attendance upon Harold Carobleat at the time of *his* death six months ago.'

Mr Chubb started and puffed out his cheeks. 'Oh, look here,' he said, then subsided and murmured, 'Good Lord,' with great restraint.

'Yes, sir?' Purbright inquired respectfully.

'Well,' said the Chief Constable, 'it's only that you've mentioned this chap Carobleat several times before. If you're going to bring him up again, at least you might explain what he has to do with all this. I really don't see the connection, except through the widow woman, so to speak.'

'That is one connection, certainly,' Purbright agreed. 'But I think I also mentioned Carobleat's will, didn't I, sir?'

'Yes, you did.'

'Which only turned up fairly recently.'

'I don't remember your saying that.'

'No, sir. But that is what happened. And in view of the fact that Mr Gloss proves to have been Carobleat's solicitor as well as Gwill's, we might be forgiven for finding the unorthodoxy of the chain of events that began with Carobleat's death somewhat disquieting. Particularly'—he forestalled another interruption—'as it is fairly clear that Carobleat, Gwill, Gloss, Hillyard and the undertaker Bradlaw were originally concerned together in some enterprise that they succeeded in keeping remarkably private, but which, if I am not mistaken, was illegal.' Purbright paused, then added with the air of having given the point some consideration, 'And immoral, to boot.'

Mr Chubb looked shocked. Love, too, seemed taken aback—but rather in the manner of a schoolboy who succeeds in getting two packets of cigarettes from a kicked slot machine instead of one.

'Well, you know best what lines to work along, Purbright,' said Mr Chubb, 'but do try and keep a charitable view of these people. Until you know the worst, of course. I don't believe in sentiment where criminals are concerned. But background counts for a lot with me. Chaps don't usually go off the rails overnight after years and years of being useful and respectable citizens.'

Purbright looked up from his papers and smiled. 'No, sir,' he said. 'Some of them are off the rails all the time but manage to keep the fact to themselves.'

The telephone on the desk rang. 'Take it at the switch, will you, sergeant,' Purbright said to Love, 'and tell whoever it is I'm engaged.'

'Don't mind me, my boy,' Mr Chubb protested, but Love was already through the door and the bell did not ring again.

A few moments later, the sergeant came hurrying back into the office. His cherubic composure looked strained. 'Excuse me—sir,' he said carefully to Purbright, 'but perhaps you ought to know straight away. That was Mrs Gloss on the phone. The solicitor's wife. She says Mr Gloss is dead. Someone took a stab at him as he was coming into his house a little while ago. That is what she alleges—sir.'

Purbright looked at the Chief Constable. 'It shortens the list of suspects, anyway,' he said.

CHAPTER FOURTEEN

'But look here, Doctor, surely you have some inkling? How big was the fellow? Which way did he go?'

Mr Chubb, interrogator, was finding Dr Hillyard's granite imperturbability very difficult to scratch.

'I tell you I didn't even see him. There was just a'—he carved the air with one of his long, oar-like hands—'a dark shape right under our noses, then Gloss seemed to lift. He gave a sort of squeak, that's all, and went down outside the gate, there. Plonk. And I knelt down to see what was wrong. Aye.'

The sitting-room of the house in St Anne's Place gave the impression of being somewhat crowded, as rooms do when they contain men wearing overcoats. Actually there was no lack of space for the five people who occupied it, although one of them, the so lately late Mr Rodney Gloss, silently monopolized the whole of the large chesterfield in its centre.

Dr Hillyard sat forward in an armchair, staring morosely at the sheet that covered the solicitor's body. He stressed bony fingers in a consultative pyramid. The presence of three policemen appeared to distress him not at all.

Love was busy folding a jacket and a dark overcoat, the darker stain on which he carefully left uppermost when he placed it with other clothing on a stool.

Purbright sat on a chair arm near the window. His mop of yellow hair glinted against the background of grey velvet curtains. He watched Hillyard's face with an expression that suggested kindly absent-mindedness.

From his instinctively adopted post near the fireplace, the Chief Constable threw out another question. He sounded a fraction peeved and incredulous.

'You say this assailant made no sound whatever, doctor? Said nothing?'

'Nothing.'

'Not a word to either of you?'

'He didn't ask to be introduced, if that's what you mean.'

'That is not what I mean, doctor,' said Mr Chubb coldly. 'It simply seems extremely odd that murder is committed in a residential area of Flaxborough with the technique, as it were, of an oriental assassin.'

Hillyard made no reply.

Purbright asked him gently: 'How do you account for the blood on your own clothing, sir?'

'See if you can turn over a man with a heart wound and stay clean,' retorted the doctor.

The inspector nodded as if satisfied. 'What sort of a blow would you say had been used? Powerful, of course?'

'Quite powerful. A deal of cloth had to be penetrated.'

'And a body.'

'Aye—that too.'

Purbright stood up and stepped over to the walnut table near the Chief Constable. He bent and examined, without touching, the long knife that lay there on a sheet of brown paper.

'It would be no use asking if you had seen this before?'

'No use whatever,' confirmed Hillyard.

Purbright went back to his perch. 'When and where did you meet Mr Gloss this evening, doctor?'

'He called shortly after surgery. About nine, I should guess. We talked awhile over a whisky or two.'

'It wasn't a professional call?' put in the Chief Constable.

'From what aspect, may I ask? Medical or legal?'

'Either.'

'No.'

'Would you care to tell us what object Mr Gloss had in calling to see you, sir?' Purbright sounded less insistent than Mr Chubb.

'His objects, I suppose, were exercise, liquor and conversation, in that order. He achieved all three in moderation. I might add—in case misleading theories are burgeoning in your mind, inspector—that our talk was innocent, trivial and unsuggestive of violence.'

'How long did he remain at your home?'

'An hour, maybe. We left say twenty minutes before his wife called you on the telephone.'

'And walked directly here?'

'Directly. But in no haste.'

'Why did you accompany him, sir? It's not a particularly pleasant night for walking.'

'Is it not? I hadn't noticed.'

'By the way, doctor, did you have a fairly busy surgery this evening?'

Love looked quickly at Hillyard, who replied: 'My surgery is always busy. Disease is like crime, inspector: there is a constant concentration of it in society everywhere.'

'Both will respond to treatment, though?'

'Aye—to a strictly limited degree.'

'Yet perseverance is still worth while. Is that why you provide special clinical facilities at your house, Dr Hillyard?' Purbright's expression was one of earnest encouragement.

'Is that point . . . ah'—Hillyard grappled for a word—'germane—aye, germane—to your inquiries, inspector? Tell me that, will ye?' The emergence of the accent put sardonic challenge into the words. He held his head forward and askew, like a bird's.

Purbright let the retort go by. 'You were acquainted, I believe, with the late Mr Gwill?'

'I was.'

'And with the late Mr Carobleat, who lived next door to him?'

'I have been acquainted in my time with many citizens now deceased, inspector. As a doctor, I doubt if I am unique in that respect.'

'I don't suppose you are. But it is possible that your special knowledge might help us to dispose of some rather odd coincidences and the sort of rumours that always follow them and hamper us in our work.'

Dr Hillyard spread out his hands and smiled wryly.

'You attended Mr Carobleat—we might as well proceed in chronological order—and signed a death certificate in respect of pneumonia and heart failure. That is so, doctor?'

'To the best of my recollection.'

'The illness was quite short?'

'Short—but conclusive.'

'And you have no reason, looking back now, to doubt the accuracy of your findings?'

'None whatever. Why should I?'

'What is your opinion, doctor, concerning the death of Mr. Gwill?'

Hillyard shook his head. 'I have no knowledge of that. I'm sure your own police surgeon could give you more help than I can.'

'I wouldn't say that, sir. After all, you were in Mr Gwill's company until very shortly before he died.'

Hillyard regarded Purbright narrowly for a few seconds. Then he said: 'I suppose you are indebted—posthumously'—he glanced at the sheeted form in the centre of the room—'to Gloss for that information?'

'You were present that night, then?'

'It was a social occasion, simply. Of the sequel, if whatever happened to Gwill can be called a sequel to a little informal conversation and a drink or two, I know nothing. Gloss will have told you that Gwill received a telephone call from someone or other and left the house. We did not see him again.'

'You did not gather who made the call?'

'No.'

'What did you and Gloss do when Gwill failed to return, doctor?'

'We waited perhaps half an hour and then went home.'

'Was no one else there at the house?'

'No, I think not. The housekeeper was away for the night.'

'But, doctor'—Purbright leaned forward—'Gloss told me that Mr Bradlaw was there also. He arrived in his van, surely. And all three of you came back to town in it together. That is so, isn't it?' He watched for the effect of the guess.

'Of course,' said Hillyard, blandly. 'That's what I told you myself not half a minute ago.'

The inspector stared at him. 'I beg your pardon, sir. Bradlaw wasn't mentioned until . . .'

'Nonsense, man; ye're bletherin'.'

Mr Chubb had been watching the interchange between Purbright and the doctor in a dumbly pivotal manner. He found the drift of question and answer to be going further and further, in his opinion, from the immediate problem of the solicitor's killing, and decided to bring the inquisition back firmly to the here and now.

'Had Mr Gloss any enemies, doctor?' he asked.

'He may well have had.'

'Really?' Mr Chubb was temporarily disconcerted. 'Why do you say that?'

'He was a solicitor. The profession does not attract draughts of the milk of human kindness.'

'I see. But do you know of anyone specifically who wished him harm?'

'I can think of no one in particular.'

The Chief Constable was about to put another question when there was a sound of a vehicle drawing to a stop outside the house. Love hurried to the door and returned to announce the arrival of an ambulance, Dr Hooper, the police surgeon, and a photographer. Soon the room seemed more indecently overcrowded than ever. The Chief Constable managed to draw Purbright aside, asked him somewhat superfluously if he could 'manage', and escaped.

Half an hour later, Dr. Hillyard having been dismissed with a polite injunction to be ready for further unavoidable demands upon his patience, Purbright and his sergeant were left in an empty house by the departure of corpse, police surgeon and photographer. Mrs Gloss had been collected much earlier by a shocked but comforting brother-in-law with a car.

Purbright, deservedly resting in the depths of an armchair, looked at Love and sighed. 'The doctor?' he asked.

Love gave the slight grunt that he used to acknowledge axiomatic situations. 'No one's going to tell me,' he said, 'that he would know what his own pal's assailant looked like—if there really was an assailant. There's a street lamp almost directly outside, and that's where Gloss was knifed. Incidentally, you'd think that whoever stabbed him must have got his sleeve pretty wet.'

'As Hillyard did,' Purbright put in.

'That's what I mean. The bloke's a villain; it stands out a mile.' Love was pinkly indignant. 'I'd like to bet you anything you like he did Gloss *and* Gwill.'

'In that case,' Purbright said thoughtfully, 'we might not be very far wrong in wondering if he had a hand in another little matter much earlier on.' He put one leg over the chair arm and lit a cigarette. 'You know, Sid, the death that we ought to have looked into before now is one that passed off nicely with a respectable certificate, a quiet funeral and not a single question.'

'Carobleat's, you mean?'

'Of course. Carobleat's. As you'll have gathered by now, Carobleat's activities were almost certainly crooked; some of them, anyway. Behind that broker-age firm of his were several lines of business that we were trying to put a finger on at about the time he was taken ill. The excise people were convinced that smuggling was one. He had all the contracts he could want on the shipping side, and as long as he wasn't too ambitious he would have had no difficulty in dis-posing of what was brought in. He had the sense to keep it manageably modest.

'Inevitably,' continued Purbright, 'that sort of game would begin to include the more risky but much more profitable handling of drugs. That sounds a bit far-fetched, perhaps, but I'm told the odd packer finds its way into little ports like this fairly regularly. And there's the hell of a lot of money to be made out of even one small parcel.'

'Do you know that he was handling drugs?' Love asked.

'Not for certain. But it would help to explain Caro-bleat's connexion with Hillyard. As a doctor, Hillyard would have been exceedingly useful in providing cover.'

Love sat upright suddenly. 'The antiques!' he ex-claimed. 'I nearly suggested it earlier.'

Purbright shook his head. 'No, the antiques are
something else altogether. Another Carobleat legacy,
I fancy, but nothing to do with drugs. What is interesting about the antiques, though, is that they are the
only obvious link between the late Mr Carobleat and
the late Mr Gwill.'

'Except Mrs Carobleat.'

'Ah . . .' Purbright reflected. Then he asked:
'Do you happen to know Shropshire at all, Sid?'

The sergeant frowned. 'I once went through that
was on a trip to Colwyn Bay or somewhere. When I
was a kid, that was.'

'Never mind. No, as I was saying, the antiques do
suggest connexions. A councillor's crusading zeal; the
advertising columns of a newspaper; a doctor's house;
and an undertaker who does building jobs with
promptitude and tact. What a pity so few good syndi-
cates can hang together for very long.'

Reluctantly pulling himself out of his chair, Purbright walked to the window and peered between the
curtains. 'Manning ought to be here before long. I
think he might as well come inside for the night.
There's no point in playing sentries in weather like
this.' He turned. 'By the way, did you see a phone
anywhere about?'

'Just outside this room, on a table.'

When Purbright returned five minutes later, he announced that he had rung the Chief Constable, that
Dr Hillyard would be arrested the next day, and that
they both might as well go home to bed as soon as the
tardy Constable Manning made an appearance.

'Incidentally,' he added, 'I only hope he lasts the
night'.

Love looked blank. 'Who? Manning?'

'No, Hillyard. He'll be safe once we can get him
into a cell tomorrow, of course, but passions seem to
be running high.' Purbright examined his knuckles,

then looked at the sergeant. 'What do you suggest we charge him with?'

'What, as well as doing Gloss?'

Purbright shook his head. 'We haven't enough to charge Hillyard with that. Not at the moment. But we'll have to get him into custody somehow.' He slowly paced the length of the room and stood looking at a large, slightly fly-blown engraving of a barrister ancestor of Rodney Gloss. He turned. 'I know—living on immoral earnings. How's that?'

The bewildered sergeant regarded Purbright with something like alarm.

'You do see what we're after?' Purbright asked him gently.

Love made no reply. Footsteps halted outside and there was a heavy knock on the front door. Purbright lifted a curtain aside. 'Ah, our Mr Manning,' he announced gratefully. 'Let's go home.'

As they turned out of the gate a few minutes later, Purbright said with a tinge of repentance in his voice: 'You didn't think I was pulling your leg about the immoral earnings charge, did you? It will stick, all right.'

Love grunted, and Purbright went on: 'As you'll have realized, the antiques lark, or clinic, or whatever you like to call what you very commendably uncovered this evening, is nothing but a nicely camouflaged ... er ... what should we say. . . ?'

Comprehension suddenly came upon the sergeant like the smell from a Sunday oven.

'A love nest!'

'Exactly!' said Purbright, admiringly.

CHAPTER FIFTEEN

The Flaxborough Sharms were a group of narrow and shabby streets lying between the harbour and the goods station. At one time they had enjoyed a reputation attributable to the appetites and intransigence of foreign seamen, but Continental boats seldom docked at Flaxborough now and the men from the coasters and fishing vessels that did use the port were mostly either natives of the town or regular and inoffensive lodgers in it.

Since the war, the excitements of the place had dwindled to routine drunkenness at the week-end, the odd fight or two, and a little listless wife-beating in such households where that indulgence could be enjoyed without endangering a television set.

Broad Street was in fact not a street but a quadrangle on the northern side of the Sharms. There were a few trees in the centre, a statue of a man in old-fashioned clothes who seemed stricken with impetigo (it was a cheap statue and the material 'wept' in damp weather), and a ruined horse trough. The houses on the perimeter were larger than most others in the district, for they had been built to the fancy of the retired master mariners and ship owners of a century and more ago; men who had liked to strut gravely round the little central green and sniff with proprietorial satisfaction the smells of tar, hemp and weed-slimed breakwaters. Their homes now were not so much dignified as gaunt. In their façades of faded stone, streaked brown where guttering had split, were front doors battered and scarred by the impatient passage of sub-tenants and the imprecations of over-looked and locked-out children. The imitation columns that flanked the doors had long since lost their flutings beneath an encrustment of brown paint and grease-bound dust.

Detective Constable Harper discovered with annoy-ance that the houses of Broad Street were numbered more or less at random. Only after he had trudged along three sides of the quadrangle, peering into dim hallways and cross-examining truculent infants, did he succeed in tracing the entrance of number sixteen to the bottom of a narrow court between numbers twenty-five and twenty-seven.

On the directions of a wall-eyed man in shirt-sleeves who answered his knock, Harper climbed three flights of coco-matted stairs and tapped on a door that boasted a huge white porcelain handle. Af-ter a few seconds, the door opened sufficiently to re-veal a tired but suspicious eye beneath two hair curlers that bobbed at him like wary antennae.

'Mrs Margaret Shooter?'

'You from the electricity?'

'No, madame. I am a police officer and I have rea-son to believe you can help us in a matter we are making inquiries into.'

The curlers shook vigorously. 'No, I don't think so. I've not got mixed up in anything.'

'There's no suggestion that you have, madame'—Harper remembered the inspector's tactical briefing —'but there are just a couple of questions I should like to ask you if you'd be so good as to co-operate. There's no need for you to be apprehensive, as you might say.' He gave what he hoped was a disarming smile.

'It's a bit of a liberty, but you'd better come in, I

suppose,' said Mrs Shooter, opening the door to dis-
play more hair curlers and an expanse of blue
dressing-gown.

'If I've come at an inconvenient time . . .' began
Harper, resolutely looking away from the garment's
inadequacies.

Mrs Shooter sighed impatiently; grasped his arm
and propelled him with some firmness into the room
behind her. She closed the door, flopped into an armchair and lit a cigarette. 'Now, busy boy, what's it all
about?' she looked bored as well as tired.

Harper sat carefully on the edge of a chair at the
farther side of the room.

'We are making inquiries,' he said, 'into the visits
of certain people to premises at number one hundred
and twenty, Spoongate, above a doctor's surgery. Information has reached us that you were present at
that address last evening. Would you mind confirming that, Mrs Shooter?'

She scratched her thigh and regarded him lazily.
'You're making heavy weather of something, son, but
I don't quite catch on to what it is.'

Harper sighed. He was used to extrovert females.
'Were you there last night?' he asked baldly.

'Was I where?'

'At Dr Hillyard's surgery.'

Mrs Shooter hesitated, then said: 'Yes, if you say so.
He happens to be my doctor. Any objections?'

'You are undergoing some sort of special treatment,
aren't you, Mrs Shooter? In those cubicles upstairs, I
mean.'

'Just what exactly are you getting at, copper?' Her
tiredness had evaporated. 'It's the first time I ever
heard of a busy sticking his snout into a . . . a
. . . doctor-patient relationship!'

'A doctor-patient relationship,' Harper repeated.

He gave a thin, slow smile. 'Oh, no, I wouldn't think of prying into anything like that, madame.'

She scowled and drew angrily on her cigarette. 'I don't have to answer those damn silly questions,' she reminded him.

'That's so,' he agreed, adding immediately: 'What do your friends call you, Mrs Shooter? Would it be Mabs?'

'It might be. What's that to you?'

'M. A. B. S.?'

'Of course. How would you spell it—with an X?'

Harper smiled again. Half to himself, he murmured: 'Mahogany and beech sideboard.'

This earned a look of hostile incomprehension. 'Are you all right, copper?'

He went on: 'Do you know a Mr Herbert Stamper?'

'No, I don't.'

'You didn't meet him last night? By appointment?'

'I've told you once, I went to the doctor's last night. Then I came back home. I don't know anyone called Stamper.'

Harper realized that, in spite of her denials, Mrs Shooter was not going to block his questioning altogether. He saw that she was interested. She was also apprehensive. She wanted to learn how much he knew and what use might, if the police had their way, be made of it. Yet part of her attitude, he told himself, was genuine bewilderment.

'Do you,' he asked her, 'know a girl or a woman called Jane?'

'I shouldn't be surprised.'

'Friend of yours?'

'Maybe.'

He glanced quickly at a list given him earlier that morning by Inspector Purbright. 'Japanese Antique Newel, Ebony,' he intoned softly. Mabs Shooter looked in mock despair at the ceiling.

'And what about Joan and Sal? How are they getting along these days?'

The woman said nothing.

'Superior Antique Lampsand,' murmured Harper dreamily. He put the list back in his pocket.

'How long have you and your friends been patients of Dr Hillyard's?'

'Quite a while. I have, at any rate. I don't know what friends you're talking about.'

'I think you do, you know, Mrs Shooter. In fact, I think you know perfectly well what this is all about. You do, don't you?' Harper's tone was that mixture of It's-All-Up and No-One-Will-Hurt-You-If-You-Tell that policemen use when hard evidence seems to have run out and they would give a day's pay for a nice straight confession.

'Look,' he said, leaning towards her and extending the fingers of his left hand as if in readiness to mark off five irrefutable and urgent reasons for her co-operation, 'I'm going to be absolutely frank with you, Mrs Shooter. And what's more'—he raised his eyebrows— 'I'll tell you right at the start, and with no ifs and buts, that whatever you care to tell me you'll be in the clear all the way. We'll hang nothing whatever on you personally so long as you play the game with us.'

'You'd have your work cut out,' she retorted softly. 'I know the law.'

'Of course you do. And you know we're only interested in the people who run these things. The tight lads who draw their eight quid a customer and sit back nice and safe and respectable while . . .'

'Eight quid!' He had struck fire. 'Eight quid! Don't give me that, son!' She laughed stridently, her eyes questioning and angry.

Harper glanced round the tidy, austerely furnished room. 'I don't suppose you're making a fortune, me duck,' he said.

The colloquialism pleased her, though she didn't know why. 'Not exactly,' she said.

'I'm not kidding you about the eight quid,' said the detective. 'We stopped some letters. Not that you need let that go any further.'

'Letters to the doctor, you mean?'

'He'd get his share. They took a long way round, though. All very hush-hush. You'd be surprised. But there's not much we don't know now.' Harper leaned back and searched for a cigarette. 'One thing's definite. You're going to need to change your doctor.'

'You aren't really going to knock old Hilly-billy off, are you?' she asked earnestly.

'Hilly-billy?'

'Hillyard.'

He paused in bringing up the match he had just struck. 'You should know better than to ask that,' he reproved. Then he lit the cigarette and added: 'As it happens, the warrant's out now.'

The woman digested this information. She looked straight at Harper. 'Who the hell tipped you off about me? That's what I want to know. We never even used the front door—me and the girls, I mean. And there wasn't any names mentioned. Not ever.'

'You were unlucky. Somebody recognized you. A policeman, believe it or not.'

Mrs Shooter swallowed, as though trying to push down the tide of colour that had risen round her plump throat. 'Not . . . not a bloke with a torch? Do you mean that wasn't old Bert? Oh, for crying out . . .' She jumped to her feet and glared down at Harper.

'Bert?' repeated Harper, unruffled.

She tossed her head. 'Yes, a pot-bellied old bastard. A regular. One of the life-of-the-party ones. I don't know his proper name. There was never no names. Just appointments, and initials, sort of.'

Harper sighed and handed her his cigarette case. 'Let's start at the beginning, shall we?'

She accepted a light and blew smoke to the yellowed ceiling of the little room. After a few moments' silence, she shrugged and pulled the dressing-gown more closely around her.

'That would be'—she picked a shred of tobacco from the tip of her tongue and regarded it vacantly—'about three—no, four—years ago, I suppose. One afternoon a fellow walked in here and said wouldn't I like a decent regular job instead of what I was doing and how he could fix it because he was on the council and thought it wasn't really my fault but the district I lived in. You know the gaff. I was green, considering, mind. And could he gab? Well, you must have known him yourself, I expect. Carobleat. You did? Yes . . . Councillor Godalmighty Harry Carobleat. That's who it was. Anyway, the next thing . . .'

Mrs Popplewell, the only Flaxborough magistrate who could be found willing that morning to preside over the brief formalities of a special court, sat in Purbright's office and looked with secret excitement at the charge sheet. The prisoner, she had been told by the station sergeant, would be brought in very shortly: at eleven, the inspector had said. It was now nearly five minutes past, but Mrs Popplewell had nothing in particular to do before a luncheon of business and professional women two hours hence, so she remained contentedly fingering her big green beads and easing her shoes half off under the inspector's desk, which served as a bench of justice on these occasions.

'The prisoner,' she repeated to herself in a flutter of anticipation. Dr Hillyard a prisoner. One could hardly believe it. He was such a masterful man. With iron-grey hair—yes, that was the word, iron-grey—and penetrating eyes. Dour, perhaps, but that was because

he was Scotch. Scottish, rather; they preferred being
called that. And if it hadn't been for the drink, they
said, he'd be in Harley Street today. But what a
shocking thing he was supposed to have done. A
disorderly house. It sounded comic in a way. People
went to Dr Hillyard with disorders and now his house
had caught one. No, it wouldn't do for her to giggle
while she was asking him if he had any objection to
being remanded in custody. It was a serious business,
all right—and wouldn't it lay her lunch companions
by their ears. Half of them were probably his patients. They'd be absolutely green. . . .

The station sergeant knocked and entered the
room. 'I'm very sorry you're being kept waiting,
ma'am, but from what we hear there's been some difficulty in apprehending the defendant.'

'That's all right, constable. I'm quite comfortable,'
Mrs Popplewell assured him with a dignified smile.

The sergeant glanced meaningfully at his striped
sleeve and inquired: 'Would you happen to care for a
cup of coffee, ma'am? I can easily send one of the
constables out for one.'

Mrs Popplewell reddened slightly and said it was
most kind of him but she would rather not. Was
there, by the way, any suggestion of the, er, defendant
being out of town or anything?

The sergeant said he could not speak as to that,
but no doubt the inspector would soon be back, with
or without the prisoner, and she could then ask him
the reason for the delay.

Purbright in fact appeared a few minutes later. He
wished Mrs Popplewell good morning, ran his fingers
through his hair and rubbed his chin. 'We seem,' he
told her, 'to have been a little premature in asking
you to come along. I'm terribly sorry.'

'Not at all,' she said, hiding her disappointment in
an unnecessary search for her handbag which lay just

at her elbow. 'You cannot help it if people beat you to the draw, as it were.' She laughed and added as casually as she could contrive: 'Where's he off to, do you think?'

'That's rather hard to say. All we know is that he is not at his home and, according to his receptionist, not on his rounds, either. But he'll turn up, Mrs Popplewell; don't you worry.'

It was, of course, Purbright who was doing the worrying. He reproached himself for not having gathered up the doctor the night before. There was enough trouble afoot without having to use his limited resources on one of those sordid and time-wasting searches of empty buildings, hedges and ditches, harbours, rivers and canals. Dragging . . . he shuddered at the thought.

Reluctantly, Mrs Popplewell took her leave.

Purbright made one or two telephone calls, then went outside again and started the car. He was driving off when he caught sight of Love, crossing the road towards the police station.

'No luck?' Purbright asked.

Love shook his head and climbed into the passenger seat.

'Not only that,' he said, 'but another one's gone as well. Bradlaw isn't there. His housekeeper or whoever she is told me he went out early in the van. He didn't say where or why.'

'Had Hillyard been there, did she know?'

'She said she didn't hear anyone else.'

'Never mind. Stay with me now and we'll go over to Gwill's place and the wily widow woman's. I've asked for a watch to be kept for Hillyard's car. Oh. . . .' He paused in the act of releasing the hand-brake and opened the car door. 'Hang on a minute; I'd better tell them to look for Bradlaw's wagon as well, now.'

When he returned, Love asked: 'Why should the pair of them be making a break—if that's what they are doing? Hillyard can't know about that warrant and we've nothing on Bradlaw.'

The inspector shrugged. 'The more the corpses, the closer the survivors will stick together. That particular board of directors has narrowed considerably of late.'

The car turned into Heston Lane and sped past the tall villas behind their hedges of evergreen and the mournful laurels. As it slowed just before the last two houses, Purbright said: 'You'd better see if you can root any sense out of the Poole woman, Sid. I'll try next door.' They got out. Purbright left Love regarding the now closed gates of The Aspens.

A moment later he stopped in his tracks to Mrs Carobleat's porch. Love had called out loudly and excitedly. Purbright frowned and walked back to the road. He was met by the sergeant, glowing and gesticulating. 'Don't froth,' said Purbright testily. He found demonstrative policemen as embarrassing as sentimental lawyers, or muscular clergymen.

Love led him back to The Aspens. They entered the drive and turned. Love pointed to the handle that lifted the latch securing one wrought-iron gate to the other.

'Where have you seen that before?' he asked in cryptic triumph.

Purbright grunted and bent down to look more closely at the handle.

The iron had new, bright rust upon it where it had been scraped or rubbed clean fairly recently. It was wheel-shaped and about three inches in diameter. The spokes were decorative and formed a flower pattern, rather like a daffodil.

'Yes,' said Purbright, standing up. 'Yes, indeed.' He began examining the rest of the iron-work from the central leaf to the heavy timber pillars that supported the gates.

At the top of the right-hand gates, near the wooden post and on a level with his head, he found another scarlet patch of recent rust. He pointed it out to Love and said: 'Here's where Gwill's volts were introduced, Sid. And here'—he made as if to grasp the iron daffodil with his other hand—'is where they were delivered.'

'Just what I thought,' said Love. 'That's why I . . .'

'Of course,' said Purbright. 'You were quite right to mention it.' He gazed at the hedge that divided the front garden of The Aspens from its neighbour. 'A cable run along that and clipped to the top of the gate. It couldn't have been spotted in the dark. Probably not in daylight, for that matter. The question is, Which house was it led from? Gwill's or Mrs Carobleat's?'

Followed by Love, he moved slowly along the side of the hedge, scrutinizing the frost-hardened earth beneath it. About half-way along, he saw a glint of bright yellow among the dead twigs and leaves. He picked up a short length of adhesive wrapping tape and carefully removed the fragments that were sticking to it. He pressed the adhesive side down on a page of his notebook and showed it to Love.

The piece of tape had been cut off through three lines of printing, leaving—NWELL LTD. at the top,—IO AND TV below it, and—DLOW at the bottom.

As they were looking at it, a voice just behind them croaked with querulous sadness: 'Have you come to stake him down? Have you, sir?'

The policemen wheeled round and stared into the grey, unhappy face of Mrs Poole.

'Good morning,' said Purbright with automatic courtesy. Then, realizing the oddity of her question, 'Have we come to what?'

She looked at him for several seconds and shook her head doubtfully. 'No,' she murmured, 'no, I suppose that's not your job. But somebody ought to. You'd never have thought their hair would keep growing, would you? But it's natural enough, really, I expect.'

'Yes,' said Purbright, uncomfortably, 'I suppose it is.' He noticed the woman looked much older out of doors. Her features seemed far more ravaged than when he had last spoken to her.

Mrs Poole passed a trembling, skinny hand over her little pursed mouth. 'It wasn't here, you know,' she said. Tilting her head, she added: 'Round the back, as a rule. Except when he fixed up the wireless just before I went to Libbie's.' She giggled weakly and a tear started to slide down the grey curtain of her cheek.

Purbright gave Love the flicker of a glance, then took Mrs Poole by the arm and led her back towards the front door. He held his head low and spoke to the ground. 'Libbie's your sister, is she?' he asked. She nodded emphatically.

'So the wireless was fixed that morning—was that it?'

'Early on. Only just light. Only . . .' She spoke dreamily, groping for words.

'You saw something, then, did you, Mrs Poole? Something out here?'

'I was getting up, you know. You look out of a window and there you are. You're never the first. Not in winter, even. Mind you'—she suddenly looked at him sternly and spoke low and fast—'mind you, it's my opinion he was never far away all night, so it was small credit to him to be there, already up and whiskery and busy with his aerial over the hedge to get the eight o'clock news.' She snorted and rubbed her hands on her pinafore.

Purbright stopped in front of the porch and faced the housekeeper. 'Who, Mrs Poole?' he asked. 'Who was it fixing the wireless that morning?'

She slowly drew up a hand and began fingering her chin with little fluttery movements. She made no answer, but moved back to the door, staring at Purbright as she retreated. Just before she disappeared, she announced with dignified lucidity and a fleeting smile: 'Mr Gwill keeps rather to himself these days, but I shall tell him you called.'

CHAPTER SIXTEEN

The man behind the wheel of the squat black van was not fond of driving for its own sake, even in the rolling dairylands of the Westcountry that contrasted so strongly with the utilitarian, arable flatness that surrounded Flaxborough. He glared despondently through the windscreen at the unpredictable road ahead, snaking between high banks bearing their rain-heavy tangle of dead cow parsley, vetch and spear grass. To his companion he said not a word.

It was still light enough to see Clee Hill crouching like a lonely old sheep-dog in the mist away to the left. On the near side of it, a small forest of skeletal trees held tapering, motionless fingers against the slate-coloured sky. The occasional road-side cottage, withdrawn against a leafless, dripping orchard or standing amidst a forlorn garden of soured, broken potato plants and stripped brussel stalks, showed no sign of occupancy. Here was a landscape gone to seed and bedded down to rot quietly until spring.

At the next cross-roads, Dr Hillyard steered the van carefully to stop against the verge and studied a map. He also drank gratefully from a silver flask and lit a cigarette. Then he checked the map with the signpost and drove off into the right-hand turn.

The road descended steeply through a dank plantation and drew level beside a stream. This was crossed by a humped bridge that carried the road to the be-

ginnings of a village. Before entering its main street,
flanked by a hall, some stonebuilt houses and a couple of shops with lighted windows, Dr Hillyard chose
a sharp left turn and drove slowly past an inn, a farm
entrance and a long, low wall that appeared to enclose the grounds of a manor house, the chimneys of
which topped a huge yew hedge at the end of some
rough pasture.

About half a mile farther on, the road forked. At
the junction was a triangular patch of asphalt and on
it a telephone kiosk. Again Dr Hillyard pulled up.
This time he got out of the van, crossed to the kiosk
and entered it. He took a piece of paper from his
pocket and compared what was written on it with the
dial of the telephone.

Mr Bradlaw watched from his van's passenger seat.
He shivered in the chill dampness that crept through
the floorboards and slid round the cab's windows and
doors. His legs tingled and ached. Disentangling them
from the rug he had wrapped around him, he opened
the door and climbed heavily to the road as Hillyard
shouldered his way out of the kiosk.

'Well?' said Bradlaw, stamping his feet.

'That's the number, all right,' Hillyard said. He
stared up one of the roads. 'It'll not be far from here.
A cottage is the best bet. Not in the village, though.'

Bradlaw looked unhappily at the sky. 'We'll have
to be starting back inside another couple of hours,
whether we find anything or not. We should have
waited for her coming again and one of us followed
her.'

Hillyard ignored this observation. Puckering his
face so that his splayed teeth stood out from his
mouth like a bundle of piano keys, he goggled searchingly along the left-hand fork. 'Not too promising,'
he said at last. 'We'll take a look at the other one
first. You'd better drive from now.'

They had not gone far, however, before the road narrowed into a lane. Becoming progressively rougher, it eventually petered out into a track, deeply rutted by cart wheels. The only habitation in sight was a group of farm buildings, about a quarter of a mile away. Bradlaw pulled up. 'They look a dead loss.' He nodded towards the huddle of barns and outhouses.

'Aye. Well, try the other.'

Bradlaw backed the van off the track into the furrowed but firm earth alongside and, with some lurching and several stalls, managed to turn it back towards the junction. 'How anyone could live in a bloody wilderness like this . . .'

'It has its advantages,' observed Hillyard, a trifle bitterly.

The other fork obligingly remained metalled for the first half mile or so and seemed likely to continue. At the first sight of a dwelling, a small two-storey brick house on the left, Bradlaw slowed down almost to a halt. 'What do we do? Look in?'

'No. Pull up at the gate and sound the horn. Be ready to drive off as soon as we see who comes out.'

The sudden blare of the hooter rent the silent, moisture-laden air like the cry of an impaled bull. There was an almost immediate scampering and scraping and five children appeared round the side of the house. At the same time, a curtain was drawn back at one of the upper windows and a fat, wild-eyed woman stared out. Bradlaw precipitately let in the clutch and the van shot forward.

'Heaven preserve us!' murmured Hillyard, devoutly.

They had gone nearly as far again before another house came into view. It was a low-built cottage, thatched and ivied to such a degree that its windows were like the eyes of a castaway, peering through

hair. The place was only noticeable at all because of
the double gates that stood across the path turning in
from the road. These were of a sickly sienna, highly
varnished.

The cottage, or what could be discerned of it under
the multitude of ivy ropes, was of plastered brick.
The front door had a porch and a flagged path led
through the undergrowth of the neglected garden and
round the side of the building. Rank elder bushes,
trees almost, crowded to the thatch on the right-hand
side. Behind was the dark tracery of a group of tall
oaks.

Bradlaw, who had stopped the van level with the
incongruous gateway, pointed to a broad, low shed
some twenty yards to the left of the cottage. 'Garage,'
he said.

Both men surveyed the scene from where they sat.
Although the light was fading fast, no lamp had been
lit in the cottage. Nor was there any smoke from the
great ivy-strangled stack.

'Try the horn,' commanded Hillyard tersely.

The bellow echoed from the steep hillside beyond
the cottage. There was no response, from children or
anyone else.

Hillyard stared intently at the gates, then at the
shed. He wound down the window on his side, stuck
out his head and looked back along the road, then
forward in the direction the van faced.

He opened the door and jumped down. 'I'll take a
chance and look inside. You can see far enough both
ways to give me a pip if anything comes along.'

Bradlaw looked at him anxiously. 'I'd not do
that—not just walk up to it. You can't be sure that
nobody's there.'

Hillyard seemed not to hear. Before opening the
gate, he turned and said, 'You'd better stand in the

road. And for God's sake don't forget to sound that
blasted hooter if you see a car turn down this road.'

Bradlaw obediently left his seat. Glancing at the
tall, lank figure of the doctor already advancing in a
sort of athletic creep towards one of the cottage windows, he took up sentry-go for the length of his van.
At last, made nervous by the crunch of his own footsteps, he halted and continued the vigil by turning
his head this way and that and listening.

Hillyard reached the cottage and peered cautiously
over the nearest window-sill. The room within was
dark and at first he could distinguish only the pieces
of furniture immediately in front of him. There was
a console radio and a cabinet on which stood a decanter and glasses. A chair, a small table . . . As
his eyes grew accustomed to the dimness, he picked
out a broad maplewood couch, another cabinet of
some kind and two pullman armchairs facing the fireplace. The fitted carpet of pale coffee colour was re-
lieved by a single heavy rug in black and turquoise.

The room on the other side of the front door
proved to be a bedroom, apparently furnished no less
expensively, although the nearly drawn curtains limited the view from the window to about a third of its
area. The bed covers, Hillyard noticed, lay as they
had been turned back, although a suit of pyjamas
had been folded and placed on a nearby chair.

Observing, as he passed, that both front and back
doors were secured not by country latches but with
Yale locks, Hillyard walked silently round the cottage.
On all sides, decaying vegetation straggled almost to
the wall. There was the smell of perpetually wet
stone, of leaves and fungus.

The two windows at the back both gave into the
same room, a fairly narrow one that extended the
breadth of the cottage. It contained modern kitchen
fittings, except that the sink had no taps. At one end

was a small dining table and chairs. Beside the gas
stove stood a large cylinder. There were a few dishes
on the table, and also a jug and a packet of corn-
flakes.

Hillyard gave the back door a perfunctory shake. It
was locked. He returned to the van.

'That's it, all right,' he said to Bradlaw, who had
got back into the driving seat and was rubbing the
chill out of his plump knees. 'And very nicely set up.
Damn me! Very nicely. Aye!' He gave the cottage a
baleful look as Bradlaw started the engine and the
van jerked away.

'How do you know?' asked Bradlaw, switching on
the side lamps and leaning nearer the windscreen.
This was the worst time for driving, neither light nor
dark. 'How do you know it's the one?'

Hillyard lit a cigarette and ignored the question.
He was thinking. Suddenly he nudged his companion's arm. 'Quick, into there.' He pointed to a clearing by the road's edge almost immediately ahead.
Bradlaw braked and swung the van sharply round to
the right. A tree loomed up. He stopped just short of
it and swore.

'Fine,' said Hillyard. He turned and groped behind
him in the dark interior of the van. The small leather
case that he found there he thrust into his overcoat
pocket. Then he opened the door.

Bradlaw seized his arm. 'What are you going to do?'
he asked, nervousness thinning his voice.

Hillyard looked over his shoulder as he stepped
down. 'Do?' he echoed. 'I'm coming with you, friend.
You didn't think we could leave the van outside the
gate, did you? It will be safe enough here until we
want it.'

'Look here,' said Bradlaw, opening the door on his
side and clambering out clumsily, 'I thought that as
. . .' He came round the front of the van, breath-

ing quickly. 'I thought there wouldn't be anything for us to do now. With there being no one there, I mean.' He stared hopefully at the other's slightly contemptuous smile. 'Well, there isn't, is there?' His arms flapped for a moment, then he pushed both hands into his pockets and hunched his shoulders. Still Hillyard said nothing. Bradlaw glanced round at the stockade of leafless trees within whose damp gloom they stood concealed from the highway.

The doctor took his arm, not ungently, and said, as if speaking to himself: 'The time is past for pretence. That's too dangerous now. We need to make the legend a reality, or God knows when we'll sleep again.' Then he grinned in the dusk and added sharply: 'And so, my tubby little meat packer, let us go to redress an ancient wrong.'

Together they regained the road and began walking back the way their van had come. The figures in the thickening dark were like those of Don Quixote and his fearful squire.

CHAPTER SEVENTEEN

The landlord of the Brink of Discovery was not a local man but a former singer from the North of En-
gland who had saved the proceeds of brief but
phenomenally profitable popularity and invested
them in what he called 'the mine host racket.'

'You see how it is,' he said to Purbright and his
companion. 'The locals haven't enough honest thirst
to keep the flippin' beer engine from rusting. Do you
know what they do? They brew some filthy liver-lifter
of their own and guzzle it in bed until they're in the
mood to get up and fire a few ricks. What? You'd
never believe. Honest, you wouldn't. And they're all
related, this lot are. Here, even when they bother to
get married there's no call for half of 'em to change
their names. My Freda says: "There's another three
village idiots going to church" every time the
wedding bells ring. They're a bright lot round here,
I'll tell you.'

'We were hoping . . .' Purbright put in.

The landlord poddled him in the shoulder with
one finger. 'So you see,' he went on relentlessly,
'there's nothing round here to keep a pub's brass polished. They're not civilized. Arson and incest, them's
their hobbies, my Freda says, and that's just about it.
Well, if I had my way I wouldn't have 'em in the
place. They just sit around and keep spitting in their
beer to make it last out and gouging holes in the bar

floor with their ugly great boots. Look, now—look
over there at that trestle—one of 'em's been hacking
at it with a bloody scythe. I tell you they bring
scythes in here. They do—no, really.'

Seizing the opportunity for speech that seemed to
be presented by the landlord's brows rising so high
that his eyepouches were pulled taut like grey elastic,
Purbright tried again.

'We're . . .' was all he managed.

'You're dicks—yes, I know.' The landlord beamed
upon them like a school matron. 'It's those raincoats.
Here, I expect you're after one of these straw-chewing
zombies for slipping a hunk of rat poison into his
auntie. That's a favourite of theirs, rat poison is.
Some of 'em get used to it. No, you'd not believe that,
would you? But it's right. They eat it like bloody
sandwich spread. Never mind'—he tossed his head—
'we'll not waste time talking about that lot, shall we.
I was telling you how I came to make this place pay.
D'you know where the real trade comes from? The
real money? Do you?' He leaned nearer, filling the
little service hatch with his affable moon-face. 'From
the city. Brum. And over from Shrewsbury, some of
'em. And Stafford an' all. Even Liverpool in the summer. You know why, don't you? Listen. It's what we
call a gimmick in show business. A gimmick, that's
what. Like echo chambers and crimpy hair and wal-
loping great fat chests and that. You see, I got my old
agent to come and give the place the once over when
I took it on. First thing he did was change the name.
The Bull, it used to be. We'll give 'em Bull, he says.
You want something classy and half-sloshed like,
that'll go down with the intelligentsia out with one
another's missuses. Mind you, it's all above board. No
Mr and Mrs Smith or any of that lark. Proper names
and all different. Aye, anyway . . . But look here,
you're the pollis, aren't you? You'll be wanting to

know something, I suppose. Come on, don't be bashful. Hey, Freda! Freda, love!' He disappeared.

Purbright's companion blew out his cheeks and softly suspired an appropriate obscenity. 'Sorry about him, old chap, but he's not one of our home-reared, believe me. My chief just asked me to help you with the geography and the language; we didn't bargain for a blasted walking public address system.'

A door opened behind them and they were joined by the landlord, bearing a tray set with three glasses. 'Here,' he said. Purbright and the other policeman each took a whisky. 'Right,' said the landlord. He sat down and regarded them with the air of a grocer ready to take a list. His furious loquacity seemed to have burned itself out.

In the hatch vacated by the landlord suddenly appeared the face of a heavily breathing, youngish woman with lemon-coloured hair. She gazed at them with a mixture of interest and amusement. 'Lookin' for corpsesez?' she asked.

The landlord flapped his hand at her. 'Go switch the log on in the Tudor,' he commanded. His wife wrinkled her nose and lumbered off into the interior. 'Miss Openshaw Palladium 1946,' he explained, then, half to himself. 'That was before wide screens, mind.'

Purbright made formal introductions and began putting his questions.

'We're interested in a roundabout way,' he said, 'in a lady from Flaxborough—you know where that is, I suppose?—called Mrs Joan Carobleat. Has anyone ever stayed here under that name?'

The landlord yelled 'Freda!' and added in normal tones, while the glasses still quivered, 'Aye, I get you. Wait till she brings the book.'

Once more his wife materialized, Judy-like, in the hatch. 'The book, love—fetch it here, will you?' Again she was gone, good-naturedly contemptuous and foot-dragging. Purbright and the local inspector each received the distinct impression that she had winked at him.

The landlord quickly found the signature he was looking for. He held out the book and pointed to it. Purbright saw that it was for the two nights before his encounter with Mrs Carobleat as she was leaving Flaxborough station. It confirmed her own story.

'You're sure she actually stayed here—slept here, I mean?' he asked.

'Oh, yes, rather do I. I noticed, you know. She's not exactly a stranger here, if you know what I mean.'

'And there's no doubt she could have been nowhere else but here in the hotel on that second night?'

'Not unless she climbed out of the window and climbed back again in time for six-thirty tea. Look—it's marked here—tea, six-thirty. She left to catch the eight-five at Hereford.' The landlord slammed the book shut and jutted his face forward. 'What's up? What's she done? I'll not, er . . . you know. Here, don't tell me she's been minced or something?' The last question was delivered with hopeful interest and a manual gesture suggestive of sawing.

Purbright said: 'She stayed here fairly regularly, then? How often?'

'Oh, once or twice a month, maybe.'

'As often as that?' Purbright sounded surprised.

'Oh, aye. Recently, anyway. Of course, I've not been here all that long.'

'Since when?'

'Early last summer. May or June. She's been here eight or nine times since then. Just for the odd night or two.'

'And always on her own?'

The landlord hesitated.

'Well?' Purbright's tone was inoffensive, yet pressing.

The other scratched his ear. 'Put it this way,' he said. 'She was on her own all right when she was actually here. But she generally pushed off early in the evening and turned up again for breakfast. Oddly enough, though, this last time she did stay the night just as I told you. You needn't worry about that. But most other times she didn't.'

'What was the idea? Did she tell you?'

'She didn't say anything, but I thought the same as anyone else would. She's no chicken, but goodish looking. Married for a cert. And probably with a husband who'd want to know where she'd been. Well, if ever he came here he could see she'd spent the night very respectably in a single room with none of that Mr and Mrs Smith malarkey.' He shrugged. 'I didn't see any harm in obliging her. There was nothing common about her.'

'Do you know where she went when she left for the night?'

'No idea at all, old man. It wasn't my business.'

'Come off it.' For the first time, Gibbins, the local inspector, entered the conversation. 'This village is no bigger than my backside. Anyone coming here wouldn't have a dozen houses to choose from to stay the night in. Somebody's bound to know where the woman went. And I know as well as you do that the gossip out here is spread in the bars like sawdust. Now just you tell this gentleman what you've heard, my lad.'

The landlord glanced resentfully at Inspector Gibbins's whisky. 'I tell you I didn't tittle-tattle with the peasantry,' he said. 'They always keep to the Smugglers' Browserie—what used to be the bar—ever since we did the place out and stopped them trying to bring goats along with them. Percy always serves

them, not me.' He trotted to the hatch, evidently a
sort of control centre, and shouted, 'Per-CEEE!'

The summons brought forth, after a minute or so,
a huge, droopy-chopped mental deficient who kept
wringing an imaginary dish-cloth and shaking his
head. Persistent but kindly interrogation by Gibbins
won the news that the 'lady from away' had been seen
more than once bound in the direction of Avery
Woodside, but that none knew precisely upon whose
bed 'them pretty 'aunches do 'ave steamed.'

Inspector Gibbins seemed satisfied and dismissed
the mountainous haunch-fancier with thanks. He
asked Purbright if he wished to know anything further.

'Was Mrs Carobleat never in the company of anyone here? Did you never see her strike up a conversation over a drink, say, or accept a lift in a car?'

The landlord was certain that he had not.

'Did you know her to make a telephone call at any
time?'

She made no calls herself, but at her request he
had occasionally rung for a taxi or to confirm the
time of a train.

When the two policemen left the hotel, Gibbins
pointed along the road to their left. 'Avery's that
way,' he said. 'I didn't try to drag anything more out
of Perce because what he did say leaves us with a very
short choice. Come on.'

They soon drew level with a farm entrance. 'Nothing there,' said Gibbins. 'There's just the old man
and his sister and a stockman who lives in. They
don't know anybody.'

'What's that place?' Purbright asked, nodding
towards a house set in wooded grounds behind a wall
that extended along the opposite side of the road.

'Do you have squires in your part of the world?'

Purbright shook his head. 'Hardly. Our upper crust

sank into the gravy quite a while since. Why, is that a
manor? In the feudal sense, I mean?'

'It is. And wheezing in the middle of it somewhere is a real squire.'

'Paralysed with a surfeit of *droit de seigneur*?'

'Poxed and well-nigh boxed,' confirmed Gibbins. 'I
doubt if your Mrs Whatshername would have wanted
to see him; not unless she had an interest in morbid
pathology.'

'We're not calling, then?'

'Only if we have no luck farther on.'

They reached a road fork, in the centre of which
stood a public telephone kiosk.

'That's just a track,' Gibbins said of the right-hand
lane. They entered the other and began to walk more
briskly. Neither spoke until they came within sight of
a small house of red brick.

Gibbins said "We'll have a word with Mrs Battle.
Considering the number of kids she has, I wonder she
has time to notice anything that's not on the stove or
the clothes line, but it's amazing how much she finds
out. Perhaps Battle tells her. She's not been this side
of her gate since old Kennedy dropped dead from his
delivery van in the road here one Thursday morning
just after the war, and she came out and stepped over
him to get the bread she'd been waiting for.'

Walking round the side of the house, they encountered Mrs Battle picking one of the youngest of her
children out of the hen run. Purbright thought she
looked hostile and excitable, but Gibbins greeted her
familiarly and she waddled ahead of them into the
house.

After some small-talk in a dialect that Purbright
found difficult to follow but which was obviously zest-
fully indelicate, Mrs Battle began to give answers to
Gibbins's inquiries into the passage of strangers there-
abouts.

Her replies, translated one by one to Purbright by his colleague, were to the effect that a woman answering Joan Carobleat's description had indeed walked by the house on several occasions. She was a visitor, according to Mrs Battle's observations from her bedroom window, to the house of Mr Barnaby, the gentleman from London way who had bought the next cottage down the road—the last habitation before Avery Woodside—and who enjoyed such other advantages as a morning help from Polstead, a motor-car, fishing rights in the meadowlands of poor palsied Squire, and the nocturnal companionship of various anonymous but drattedly giggly young women.

Was Mr Barnaby likely to be at home now? She thought it highly probable, for she had seen the headlamp beams of his big motor-car flash across her bedroom ceiling late last night and had heard his garage door roll shut. Since then, no traffic had passed but a van or two. Mr Barnaby's big motor-car certainly had not emerged again. It made a sinful noise, as though bound for race tracks and hotels, and she would not have missed it, even in her sleep.

Had the morning help called that day, as usual? No, she hadn't, now that it came to be mentioned, not that she came absolutely every day because her husband sometimes got took extra bad.

What sort of a man to look at was Mr Barnaby? She had never looked, save at his lordly passing awheel when she had got no more than a fleet glance at his face, which was dark, she thought, and whiskered, and proud.

Whiskered? Purbright reminded Gibbins that the man who had bought electric cable from Barr and Cranwell, Ltd., Radio and TV, Ludlow, to which a fragment of yellow adhesive tape had led them earlier that day, had also been described as bearded.

How did Mr Barnaby earn a living and pass his time? She had heard nothing of his employment, but Battle thought (for what *his* opinion was worth) that their neighbour was like to be a gentleman just out of either Parliament or prison and writing a book about it.

After some further conversation in the steamy gloom of Mrs Battle's nappie-festooned kitchen, the two policemen took their leave.

When they arrived at Mr Barnaby's unexpectedly ostentatious gateway, Gibbins asked Purbright: 'Do you want to see this character on your own? He's not one of my parishioners; I might just be in the way.'

'No, you come along in,' said Purbright. 'I'm not at all sure what I'm going to say to him, anyway. At least you can fill awkward pauses by asking to see his licence, or soliciting for the Boot and Shoe Fund or something. Damn it, you can't loiter at gates in this weather.'

They made their way through the dead, tangled garden and Gibbins knocked on the front door. 'The back would be more to the point as a rule,' he observed, 'but this chap's a foreigner; he probably hasn't bothered to nail up the front door yet awhile.'

There was no sound within the cottage. Purbright knocked, again without result.

'You go round and try the back,' suggested Gibbins. 'I'll see if his car is still in the garage. It's not often old Mother Battle's espionage is at fault.' He strode off towards the shed.

Purbright knocked with his knuckles on the back door and tried the handle. Then he moved to one of the two flanking windows. Inside was a long, clean kitchen.

A few moments later, Gibbins reappeared. 'Wherever he is, he hasn't taken the car,' he announced. 'It's still in the garage.'

Purbright stared round the garden and ranged the fields on the other side of the bordering hedge. 'Curious,' he muttered.

'What is?'

Purbright nodded towards the window. 'Take a look at how neat the place is. Yet his woman didn't come today. He must be an unusually tidy fellow.'

'You'd not say that if you saw the garage. You can hardly move for odds and ends and a great tangle of electric flex and stuff. I'd a job getting the door shut again.'

'Electric flex?' Purbright looked at him sharply.

'Yes, yards and . . . Oh . . .'

'Oh, indeed,' said Purbright. 'Getting warmer, aren't we?' He turned again to the window. 'I suggest, you know, that "having reason to suspect" and all that, we now take a closer look into things.'

He examined the window frame. 'Ah, a precedent. How lucky for the Law.' Where recently made indentations appeared in the paint, he thrust upward a penknife blade and eased away the old-fashioned catch. Then he opened the window, climbed on the kitchen bench and jumped down. The slightly apprehensive Gibbins was admitted through the door.

They began to search, ascending first to an attic compartment that had been converted into the nearest approximation to a bathroom that a pumped water supply allowed.

Of the occupant of the cottage there was no sign. 'One thing to be thankful for,' confessed Gibbins, 'is that we haven't found him strung up or simmering in chunks in the copper. That's what I'm always afraid of in these out-of-the-way places. They've a nasty sense of humour in the country.' He mooched back into the kitchen and began peeping cautiously into drawers and cupboards.

A little later, Purbright called from the bedroom.

'What do you make of this?' he asked, pointing to a jacket and waistcoat that hung behind the door, and then to an open drawer of the dressing table in which had been folded the matching pair of trousers.

Gibbins moved the trousers aside. Braces were attached to them. Beneath the trousers were some underclothes and a shirt. He looked at the cuffs; the links were there. Studs had not been removed from the collar-band.

'It seems,' said Gibbins, after considering these things, 'that Mr Barnaby is abroad with precious little clothing on. People don't put on clean shirts without changing the studs over. And they don't have separate braces for every pair of trousers.'

'They don't lay trousers in drawers, either,' Purbright observed. 'Unless,' he added, 'they happen to be someone else's that they've decided to tidy away quickly. Can you see any shoes and socks over on that side?'

A pair of slightly muddied brogues was discovered in a corner. Further search revealed socks under one of the pillows. Gibbins held them up. 'Inside out— like the shirt and vest. That suggests something.'

'It does, doesn't it?' Purbright agreed, pleased that Gibbins seemed to have entered so well into the spirit of things, in spite of the case having been, as it were, imported. 'The gentleman was either an exceedingly careless dresser—which would be odd in anyone with such a passion for tidying things away—or else somebody took his clothes off for him.'

Purbright watched Gibbins going through pockets. 'Any name tags?' he asked.

'Not one. No letters, no papers. Plenty of money and some odds and ends.' Gibbins laid on the dressing table a bundle of notes, cigarette case and lighter, keys, a pen and two handkerchiefs.

'No driving licence?' Purbright inquired. Gibbins shook his head.

Purbright moved about the room, unhurriedly peering, probing, picking up and setting down. He glanced into ashtrays and the titles of a couple of books. His manner was inconsequential, like that of a bored man in a waiting-room. On the bedside table was a small china ornament. In passing, he lifted it and shook it gently, then tipped its mouth to the palm of his other hand. Out rolled a tiny, pear-shaped bead of glass. Purbright stared at it thoughtfully for a moment and slipped it into his waistcoat pocket.

Both men returned together to the kitchen.

Purbright stopped at the door and looked carefully round the room. Then he walked slowly from one end to the other, methodically examining the floor. Suddenly he stooped down and peered closely at the boards. Another piece of glass glittered in a crevice. Purbright prised it free with his fingernail, compared it with the first fragment, and held out both to Gibbins who mmm-ed politely but without comprehension.

'They're off little glass phials,' explained Purbright. 'You know—medical phials.' He stepped to the sink and surveyed the things that stood in it or on the draining bench close by; he did not touch them. They comprised a small saucepan that seemed to have contained milk; a deep plate with a few cereal fragments on its rim; a large china beaker; and an empty jug. All had been rinsed—apparently with water from a ewer that stood on the floor.

'I'd dearly like a sample of the milk that was in that jug,' Purbright said.

Gibbins stood disconsolately at the sink. 'Do you think it was poured away? It could have been used up.'

'It could; but most people remember to leave a drop of milk in reserve, and there isn't any other in the house. In any case, it stands out a mile that somebody's . . .'

'Wait a minute,' Gibbins broke in. He bobbed down and thrust his head into a small cupboard beneath the sink. 'See if you can get hold of a clean jar or bottle. A jar would be best.'

As Purbright searched shelves on the opposite wall, he heard Gibbins tapping in his retreat. He picked out a clean jam jar and handed it down. A moment later there was the sound of running liquid.

Gibbins emerged, red but triumphant, from the cupboard. He held up the jar, half filled with a whitish fluid. 'Waste pipe,' he explained. 'Now then, what do you reckon we've got here?'

'Something,' Purbright replied, 'of which I fear Mr Barnaby has caught his death.'

CHAPTER EIGHTEEN

When the Chief Constable opened the door of Purbright's office shortly after eight o'clock the following morning, something more chilly than the draught from the corridor entered the room. His terse 'Good morning' had an edge of irritation, and he said nothing further while he slowly and deliberately peeled off his gloves and laid them neatly side by side on the desk.

Purbright knew better than to waste time on mollifying preliminaries. 'I understand, sir,' he said, 'that Dr Hillyard is now at his home. I wish to execute the warrant at'—he glanced at the clock and considered—'at half-past nine. A special court has been fixed for ten. Formal remand, sir. In custody, of course.'

'Well?' Chubb had no intention of forgiving lightly the telephone call that had precipitated an early and unsatisfactory breakfast.

'Well, sir, the whole case may conceivably come to the boil, as it were, at any time now. I thought it desirable that you should be on hand. We may need your support in several ways that I cannot predict at the moment.'

Chubb regarded Purbright thoughtfully and with slightly less obvious disfavour. Then he pulled a chair to the middle of the room and sat down. 'Go on, Mr Purbright.'

'In the first place,' said the inspector, manfully coping with the novelty of addressing Chubb from above, 'I'd better give you a few more of the background facts we've been able to discover. We arrest Hillyard. Right: now there is plenty of evidence of his having allowed and, for that matter, actively helped to organize, the running of a . . . an immoral enterprise in a part of his house not accessible to his genuine patients.'

Chubb raised an eyebrow.

'The original idea was Carobleat's. He had a flair for that kind of thing—as we suspected, but couldn't prove before his death. As you know, sir, a town like this has hardly any open prostitution. Members of a small community daren't risk their reputations.

'Not so long ago, of course, the shipping trade brought seamen here who had no reason to be scrupulous, so some prostitution did exist in the harbour district. But since the war most of the ships using Flaxborough have been small coasters manned by pretty stolid types who are a poor proposition for the ladies of Broad Street. Then there was all the cleaning up agitation in the council and the local paper. Mr Carobleat was largely responsible for that, you'll remember, sir.'

'And a damned nuisance he made of himself,' confirmed the Chief Constable bitterly. 'Oddly enough, the wife tumbled to him straight away.'

'Really, sir?'

'Rather. She used to tell me many a time about his having had his "hot little eyes"—that's what she called them—all over the women on that moral welfare committee he started.'

Purbright tried briefly to visualize this mass flirtation. He failed and went on: 'What Carobleat had seen, of course, was his opportunity to reorganize the declining and amateurish vice trade on a novel, very profitable basis. He used his spurious moral welfare

approach to recruit a dozen or so of the more presentable women and promised them a regular living on
good-class clients. But he made it clear that he was to
manage the financial side himself and pay them commission. They must have found the proposition fairly
attractive—especially as he undertook to arrange the
ticklish question of premises.'

Chubb was looking doubtful. 'Just how do we come
to know all this, Mr Purbright?'

'Quite simply, sir. One of the women was interviewed by our persuasive Mr Harper. She told him a
great deal. The system was rather ingenious. She used
to receive by post at regular intervals a list of appointments, so called, together with a sum of money
in notes at the rate of a pound for each appointment.'

'In advance?'

'That's so,' Purbright agreed. 'All she had to do
then was to arrive at Dr Hillyard's surgery by the
back door just before the stated time and go straight
upstairs to what were ostensibly women's treatment
cubicles. The actual . . . er . . . assignations
took place in small rooms connecting the male and
female cubicles.'

'How abominable,' murmured the Chief Constable.

'You'll not wish me to elaborate on that particular
aspect, sir?'

'No, no. Certainly not. I'd like to know how the
others came into it, though.'

'Yes, sir. Bradlaw, now. My guess at the moment is
that he did the conversion work on the first floor of
Hillyard's house. He's a builder as well as an undertaker. We know him to have been fairly thick with
Carobleat and Hillyard, and they'd naturally want
someone who could be trusted to keep his mouth
shut. Another point. The job seems to have been
done without a licence, which would have been

needed at that time if an ordinary firm had been called in. We can assume that Bradlaw was promised a cut from the proceeds, and got it.

'As you know now, I think, sir, the fourth member of what might be called the syndicate—or the fifth, if we count Mrs Carobleat, as we must—was Gwill. Less imaginative organizers would have been content to run their business as a camouflaged brothel with nothing really elaborate about it. But these people were inspired as well as thorough.

'They knew that the best customer would be the well-off married tradesman or farmer or business man who would be only too ready to make a fool of himself as long as he could insist on the most stringent and even melodramatic safe-guards. Actually, it's often the trimmings—you know, the peephole and the password and that sort of thing—that are half the attraction for middle-aged men who dabble in vice.'

'I'll take your word for it,' Chubb remarked.

Purbright gave a little bow. 'Anyway, sir, that's where Gwill was valuable. The complicated system of coded advertisements and box replies for which his newspaper was used may seem absurd to us; after all, arrangements could have been made quite easily over the phone or through a reliable go-between. But that wouldn't have been so exciting.'

Chubb gave one of his gentle, thin smiles. 'You really are far too sophisticated for a policeman, Mr Purbright. Never mind; go on.'

'So here in Flaxborough was a flourishing and excellently organized traffic in comforts for gentlemen,' continued the inspector. 'Carobleat was the managing genius—up to last summer, that is. His next door neighbour was what you might call the public relations expert. Bradlaw won his directorship with an astute piece of construction work. Hillyard was all-important as provider of accommodation and camouflage. He might also have been useful as the M.O. of the concern—the woman we interviewed was a trifle coy on that point. And Mrs Carobleat looked after the secretarial side.'

'What about the solicitor?' asked Chubb.

Purbright thought a moment. 'Well, he certainly knew what was going on. It was he who collected that last lot of box replies, presumably to pass them on—a businesslike touch, that. I doubt if he was a regularly active partner, though. There doesn't seem to have been much he could do to help—unless we can imagine one of the ladies suing the firm for breach of contract.'

'Then why do you suppose the fellow was murdered? You don't suggest he intended to give the show away? He told me precious little, scared as he was.'

'That is one of the questions we can't answer yet, sir. My belief is that Gloss was killed for the same reason as Gwill, and by the same person.'

'Hillyard?'

Purbright shook his head. 'Hillyard was lucky that night. The blood that soaked his sleeve came from a wound in his own arm; he was holding it tightly all the time we were talking to him. That knife had been meant for him as well.'

'He might have gashed himself to give that impression.'

'In that case, he would have made no secret of the wound.'

Chubb grunted. After a pause he said: 'That leaves only Bradlaw, then?'

'On the face of it, yes. Yet I can't see him as a foot-path assassin. Whoever attacked a relatively powerful pair like Gloss and Hillyard must have been exceptionally confident and tough. It's the audacity of the thing that sounds so unlike Bradlaw.'

'And unlike Mrs Carobleat too, I suppose?'

Purbright smiled. 'Oh, yes . . . Mrs Carobleat. As it happens, she's the only one with an alibi for the night Gwill was murdered.'

'You've checked that?' A gleam of recollection showed suddenly in Chubb's face. 'Of course . . . your little trip to Shropshire. How did you get on?'

'It should prove useful, sir. For one thing, we found where Mrs Carobleat was in the habit of staying. And we learned of the existence of a gentleman called Barnaby.'

'Barnaby?'

'Yes, sir. The local people are looking for him now.'

'You mean he'll be able to help?'

'I doubt it, sir. We can but try.'

The Chief Constable looked fixedly at Purbright for several moments. 'You know,' he said slowly, 'you're hedging to a perfectly scandalous degree. No'—he raised his hand—'don't spoil it, my dear fellow; I'm sure you know what you're doing.' He rose, walked to the desk and picked up his gloves. 'There's just one little thing I must ask of you, though.'

'Yes, sir?' Purbright also was standing. He met Chubb's gaze with a politely solicitous eye.

'Arrest your murderer or murderers within the next twenty-four hours, or I shall ask Scotland Yard to give me assistance.' He reached for the door. 'I thought you should know how I'm placed. I'm the last to want some outsider to scoop the credit for what you and your chaps have done. But you do see that I cannot possibly delay any longer.'

Chubb put on his bowler with the air of an overdrawn patron of the arts and stepped into the corridor, which was darkened at that moment by the approach of the enormous Sergeant Malley.

The Coroner's Officer squeezed his bulk respectfully

to one side and allowed the Chief Constable to pass. Then he lumbered up to Purbright's door, knocked and went in.

'Ah, sergeant,' Purbright greeted him, 'I have a little commission for you.'

'Yes, sir?'

'The day before yesterday we were anxious to have a word with Nab Bradlaw. He couldn't be found. I rather think he was out of town. Now, then, you're *persona grata* with the undertaking trade, I take it—in the way of business, so to speak?'

'Bradlaw's fellows know me.'

'Fine. Well, I'd like you to try and tap somebody at his place now. See if you can find out where he went the other day. Don't scare them, though—Nab least of all.'

Malley grinned. 'You don't have to worry about that, sir. I'm pretty unobtrusive. If Ben or Charlie know anything, I'll worm it out of them.'

On his way out, Malley turned. 'By the way, inspector, do you reckon this little lot is nearly tidied up? Old Amblesby's in a terrible state. I can't do anything with him. He's like a kid who's lost his hoop.'

'Why? What's the matter?'

'Well, he's never had two inquests hanging fire at one and the same time before. There's Gwill, of course. He would have forgotten about that but for the adjournment on Gloss the other day. That reminded him. Now he's going around muttering that half the town's been murdered and his books are cluttered up with corpses.'

'Would that Her Majesty's Coroner were among them,' piously declared Purbright, closing his door.

At half-past nine exactly, the inspector and Sergeant Love presented themselves at Dr Hillyard's surgery. Purbright informed him with the greatest respect that he was being arrested and explained some of the implications of that surprising circumstance.

Dr Hillyard glowered a good deal but made no comment.

Shortly before ten o'clock, the three men entered the police station and, on a cue from the assistant clerk to the magistrates, walked into Purbright's office where Mrs Popplewell, J.P., was waiting to make the best of a redeemed opportunity. She was accompanied by a Mr Peters, a comatose draper whose shop was so near the police station that the kindness of leading him off for an airing whenever a little uncomplicated justice needed doing had become traditional.

Dr Hillyard regarded Mrs Popplewell with acid amusement throughout the brief formalities of the assistant clerk stumbling through the charge, Purbright giving evidence of arrest, and Mrs Popplewell herself announcing lamely and with every sign of nervousness that he, the defendant, would be remanded in custody for a week. Then he drew back his lips from the dog daisy of his splayed teeth and grinned a contemptuous and malevolent farewell before turning to accompany the station sergeant to the cells next to the table tennis room.

'Dear me!' said Mrs Popplewell to Mr Peters. 'And to think that his late wife was once chosen by the Association to entertain Mr Baldwin to supper.'

CHAPTER NINETEEN

'How did you make out?' Purbright asked Malley, whom he found awaiting him.

'I kept clear of Nab Bradlaw. He was busy in that chapel-cum-fridge of his. But I had a word with Ben and Charlie, and they said he'd been out with the van all that day and most of the night. Charlie lives nearly opposite the yard and he heard him coming back about five yesterday morning.'

'Did they know where he'd been?'

'No, sir; but Ben thought the van's mileage gauge had clocked on nearly four hundred.'

'He couldn't give an exact figure?'

'No, they're none too fussy about log books, it seems.'

'Will Bradlaw be there now, do you think?'

'Should be, sir. He has a job at the Crem. at twelve, though.'

'Only the one?'

'Aye, that's all. Ben was rather taken up with it, as a matter of fact. Said he'd never known things so slack in what he calls good felling weather like this. And even the one they have got was only staying here temporary, he said.'

'That applies to all of us by Nab's reckoning.'

Malley grunted.

'A visitor, was he?' asked Purbright.

'Seems he was an uncle of that housekeeper, or whatever you'd call her.'

'Bradlaw's housekeeper?'

'Yes, sir. I spoke to her, as well. She told me the same as Ben. Only the one funeral—her uncle's. He must have been ill here for a bit and under a local doctor, else they'd never have got a certificate straight off like that.'

'Was the girl upset about her uncle?'

Malley scratched his chin. 'Well, not as you might say prostrate with grief.'

'She didn't mention the man's name, by any chance?'

The sergeant shook his head, then looked thoughtful. 'Wait a bit . . . Charlie was the one who called him something. He's a bit disrespectful, is Charlie. Now what was it he said?' Malley gazed at the ceiling and made little popping sounds as if expelling invisible smoke rings.

Purbright watched him patiently for a while, then glanced at the clock. It was a little after half-past ten. He suppressed a yawn and rubbed his face.

Distracted by the movement, Malley looked down again. Suddenly he chuckled. 'That's it. Of course. Fuzzy-chops!'

'I beg your pardon?'

Malley waved a plump hand. 'No, sir. Not you. The uncle bloke. Charlie called him that. Fuzzy-chops. He must have . . .'

The inspector, uttering something between a neigh and a groan, pushed past him, seized hat and coat from the peg, and disappeared through the door.

Ten minutes later, Purbright, Love and a couple of uniformed constables descended by car upon the place of business of Mr Bradlaw.

They entered by the side gate, and Purbright and Love left the constables in the yard staring around at the stacks of elm and oak, while they went into the workshop.

At first it appeared to be empty. Then the joiner, Ben, who had been nodding in a corner until the sound of footsteps penetrated his doze, rose suddenly and bade them a challenging 'Good morning'.

'We are looking for Mr Bradlaw,' announced Purbright sternly.

Ben blinked. 'Ain't 'ere,' he retorted unhelpfully.

'Where is he, then?'

'Down at Crem., 'less he's back.'

Purbright gave Love a quick, anxious glance, then to Ben: 'Are you sure of that?'

'Course. Why not?'

'I thought he had only one funeral today.'

'S'right.'

'At eleven o'clock.'

'Was to ha' been. The missus was that upset though, they put it forrard a bit. The boss said grief like 'ers 'd take the nature out of 'er and oughter be got over quick. So that's . . .' He stopped. His audience had gone.

Those of Mr Bradlaw's near neighbours who happened to be watching the street were intrigued to see two purposeful-looking men in raincoats shoot out of the undertaker's yard, followed, but not pursued, by a pair of policemen. All four piled into the car that had brought them two or three minutes earlier, and drove away, the men in uniform crouching like big blue frogs in order to keep their helmets from penetrating the roof.

As he urged the suffering vehicle forward at what speed it would make, Purbright said to Love: 'I am a thickheaded, complacent fool.'

'I wouldn't say that,' replied Love, a little doubtfully.

'Yes, I am. If what I think has happened—and I

could have prevented it easily enough—we might as well drive straight over that parapet.'

Love stared apprehensively at the river wall on their right. 'We can only hope for the best,' he said, adding, 'whatever that may be.'

'Do you know anything about the crematorium?' Purbright asked him.

'I know what it's for.'

'I didn't suppose you imagined it was an ice-cream factory. I mean, do you know anything about the works—the procedure? Furnaces, and that sort of thing?'

'No, nothing.'

'Never mind.' Purbright stared out at the road ahead. Soon he steered the car into a broad avenue and drove between two small brick lodges. 'Here we are,' he said. 'I can get the car practically up to the door. I'll go in. There'll be a clergyman in charge, I suppose. He'll know all about what happens, if it hasn't already. You wait outside and make sure of Nab. But try not to let it look like a raid on a club—keep the *gendarmerie* out of sight unless there's any chasing. Which'—he heaved on the handbrake and drew the car to a halt on the gravel—'God forbid!'

Within the small chapel that Purbright entered with an urgent and hasty tip-toeing movement—a sort of reverent prance—were four people.

A curate from the Parish Church was murmuring a prayer with bowed head. He was being watched nervously by a young woman wearing a dark coat and a black, ill-fitting hat that she fingered from time to time as if feeling a bruise. Mr Bradlaw stood just behind her, clasping and unclasping his hands upon the tail of his coat and glancing occasionally with professional concern at the apparel and bearing of his man Charlie, whose first 'outside' assignment this was.

As Purbright looked feverishly around and tried to

judge whether he had arrived in time, there swelled
from the air above his head the sounds of music of a
Grand Hotel celestialism. It seemed to signal the end
of whatever religious rites had been in progress, for
the heads of the three people other than the curate
now swivelled all in one direction. Purbright was
aware of slow, smooth motion somewhere, yet could
not exactly place it. He studied Charlie's face, which
happened to be presented to him in profile, and followed the line of his fixed stare. He was just in time
for his eyes to catch the final phase of the movement
that the others had been watching. A coffin was de-
scending with dignified gradualness through the floor,
rather, Purbright afterwards found himself recalling,
in the manner of a cinema organ.

He strode forward. Mr Bradlaw and his housekeeper turned and stared at him. The undertaker was
very pale. The girl clutched at her hat and glanced
back towards the door. But Purbright took no notice
of either. He hurried up to the curate and touched
his arm.

'Excuse me, sir, but I am a police officer and I have
reason to . . .' He halted breathlessly and asked,
with a note of despair: 'That coffin—is it . . . I
mean, you can't fetch it up again, I suppose?'

The curate was a very young man, but he had ac-
quired a sense of occasion. Reddening furiously, he
retorted in a stage whisper: 'Really! Your suggestion
is infamous. You must leave this place immediately!'

Purbright felt completely at a loss, but he battled
on. 'Look, sir,' he appealed, 'I quite see your point.
All this must seem terribly improper, but it is most
important in the interests of justice that the . . .
the gentleman in that coffin should be held for examination.'

The curate stared. Then he acidly inquired: 'And
what, my man, do you propose to ask him?'

The inspector thrust his fingers through his hair. 'The man's dead, sir.'

'So I had presumed.'

'And the Coroner has authorized a post-mortem,' he lied. 'But that will be out of the question if this cremation is allowed to proceed. Now do you appreciate the position, sir?'

The clergyman looked thoughtful. Then he nodded, as if to signify a sudden decision, and led Purbright to a little robing room at the side of the chapel. The inspector noticed that no one else now remained in the building.

'Bit of a stunner, this, isn't it?' the curate pleasantly remarked as soon as the door had closed behind them. He groped beneath yards of cassock and offered Purbright a cigarette. The inspector, still looking very anxious, at first refused. 'Oh, don't panic,' said the curate. 'Your fellow won't be . . . these things aren't quite so immediate as people imagine. Various preliminaries, you know. But I'll go down in half a tick and make sure. I say,' he added, 'this is all in order, I suppose?'

'Perfectly,' Purbright assured him thankfully. 'Oh, yes. Absolutely.'

The curate put his cigarette, still unlit, on a shelf and opened the door. 'Hang on,' he said. 'I'll just pop down for a word with Pluto.'

He returned after two or three minutes to report that the coffin and contents were intact and awaited the disposition of Her Majesty's Coroner. 'You really must forgive my being a little gauche in these matters, but there's something terribly Sunday paperish about all this. Of course,' he added ruefully, 'I suppose you're too fearfully secret-bound to satisfy my fiendish curiosity?'

Purbright skirted the hint by asking: 'May I ask

under what name the funeral was being conducted, sir?'

'The, er, deceased, you mean?'

'Yes.'

'Well, I didn't know him personally, you know, but I believe he was the uncle of that lady you saw just now—Mr Bradlaw's housekeeper. A Mr . . .' He fished a piece of paper from a remote pocket and looked at it. 'A Mr Barnaby.'

CHAPTER TWENTY

Flaxborough's mortuary was a detached brick building, not much bigger than a garage, at the end of the
yard behind the police station. It contained two slabs,
a much battered corner cupboard raised a couple of
feet from the terra-cotta tiled floor, and a shallow
sink immediately beneath the single window. A coil
of black hosepipe, slung from a staple, looked like a
hastily scrawled charcoal circle on the flat whiteness
of the wall.

Upon the slab farther from the door, a coffin
rested. Its lid had been removed and now stood upright, propped against the cupboard.

An ancient portable gas fire coughed blue flames
from its shattered elements. The dim daylight was
augmented by an electric bulb set within a mesh
sphere in the centre of the ceiling.

Into this aseptic chamber, Purbright gently ushered
an exceedingly apprehensive-looking Bradlaw. Love
followed, and a constable, bringing up the rear, shut
the door and remained standing impassively before it.
Bradlaw glanced at the inspector, then regarded the
coffin as if searching for constructional flaws.

'Who is it, Nab?' Purbright asked quietly.

Continuing to trace with his gaze the outlines of
the box, Bradlaw avoided looking directly at the
bearded face within. 'A fellow called John Barnaby.
No one you know. He died here while he was visiting

my housekeeper. His niece. Bit of a nuisance, but there you are.' He swallowed and looked up at Purbright. 'Why? What's all this about?'

'Who gave the certificate?'

'Hillyard. He'd been attending him.'

'Referees?'

Bradlaw shrugged. 'Scott, I think. And that other chap in Duke Street. Rawlings.'

'They made no formal examination, I suppose? The usual dotted line stuff?'

'I wouldn't know about that.'

'Never mind.' Purbright's voice was friendly. 'By the way, did I tell you that Hillyard's under arrest?'

Bradlaw stared at him, slowly drawing both hands from his overcoat pockets. 'Has he . . .' he began, then was silent.

'I rather think,' said Purbright, 'that I'd better caution you before we talk any more, Nab.'

Bradlaw looked down at his hands and began to rub the knuckles of one in the other palm. He appeared to be cold.

'You are not obliged to say anything in reply to my questions, but what you do say may be taken down and given in evidence.' Purbright nodded to Love, who drew a notebook from his pocket. To Bradlaw, the inspector added: 'You can have your solicitor here if you'd rather, you know.'

Bradlaw glanced at the unoccupied slab. 'He's been here already—or had you forgotten?'

'Oh, yes, Gloss. I'm sorry.'

Purbright said nothing more for a while, but stood watching the slow, tense rubbing motion of the other man's hands. They unclasped at last and spread in acknowledgment of surrender.

'All right. I'll tell you what happened.' Bradlaw looked behind him, as if in hope of some charitable policeman having silently placed a chair there. Seeing nothing but the coldly gleaming wall, he hunched his shoulders, sighed deeply, and began.

'You may know, or you may not—I don't suppose it matters much now—that Rupert Hillyard and a few others of us were running a sort of business side-line in the town. It wasn't quite above board, if you follow me, and there were women mixed up in it. You see what . . .' He raised his eyes to Purbright. 'Perhaps you've heard already, though?'

'Yes. We know.'

Bradlaw nodded and sniffed. 'Yes, well there you are. It wasn't a thing it would have done to let out. We all had a lot to lose. Except maybe that Carobleat woman. She was quite capable of doing the stupidest things just for spite. She hated Rupert and poor old Gwill, although I always got on fairly well with her.'

'She hated Gwill? Are you sure?'

'Oh, yes. That story of her being stuck on him was just to put you off something else. Roddy Gloss thought that one up.'

'To put us off what?'

'I'll come to that in a minute. The point is that Joan was in the . . . business along with the rest of us. As a matter of fact, it was her old man who'd started it some time before he died. You didn't know that, did you? Anyway, there she was and we had to lump it. Everything would have gone nicely, even so, if only she'd kept her mouth shut. God, what a bitch!' Bradlaw grew rigid momentarily in his indignation, then dropped once more.

'You see,' he went on, 'she took up with a certain bright character in that country village of hers over in Shropshire. That's where she came from in the first place, and when her old man died she started going back for week-ends. And that'—Bradlaw jerked his head in contemptuous indication of the coffin's occupant—'is what she found for herself.'

'You mean Barnaby became her lover?'

'Lover and father bloody confessor. She told him all about what was going on here in Flax. Names and everything.'

'How did you get to know that?'

'How did we get to know! We soon knew all right when we started getting letters from the blackmailing bastard.'

Purbright raised his brows. 'He began threatening you, did he? You'd not feel too pleased about that, I expect.'

'Not as you'd notice. We tried to buy him off. Soon he was bleeding the whole thing white. You know what blackmailers are. They're worse than murderers. Even the police say that. Judges, too.' Bradlaw was gesticulating eagerly. 'One said something just last week about it being understandable that a chap had gone for the fellow who'd been screwing money out of him.'

'Cambridge Assizes,' Purbright murmured.

'Yes, that's right. Cambridge.' Bradlaw seized on the confirmation as though it were a long lost wallet. 'Well, then: you see how we were fixed. This fellow Barnaby sucking us dry from all that distance away. Poor old Hillyard nearly going off his rocker with worry. A doctor—I ask you. As for me, I didn't know what I was doing half the time.'

'And Gwill?' said Purbright, casually. 'Was Gwill worried?'

'Of course he was. Not as much as me, perhaps. I take these things very badly. But he was very upset, all the same.' Bradlaw brightened suddenly. 'That's why he did away with himself. Don't you see now? He was driven to it.'

'Was Gloss driven to it, as well?'

Bradlaw frowned. 'How do you mean? Roddy didn't commit suicide. He was killed.'

'By whom?'

'By that devil, of course.' He stretched his arm towards the coffin. 'In cold blood. That's the sort he was.'

Purbright seemed suddenly to have remembered something. 'Excuse me a minute,' he said to Bradlaw; then, beckoning to Love to follow, he walked to the door. The constable opened it. Inspector and sergeant stepped out into the yard.

A few moments later, Purbright returned alone. Facing Bradlaw once more, he produced his own notebook. 'We work on a shift system, you see.' Bradlaw, bolder now, managed to smile for a second.

Purbright unscrewed his pen. 'Right. Will you go on from what you were saying?'

'I suppose,' said Bradlaw in a lowered voice, 'you'd like me to get round to the other business now?' He glanced at the coffin.

'It's up to you.'

'Has Hillyard . . . ?'

Purbright said nothing. Bradlaw stared at him doubtfully. Then, 'Of course, he's a sick man,' he said, with the air of breaking bad news. 'You understand that. I could do nothing with him once he'd started.

'It was when Roddy was killed that he seemed to make up his mind. Up to then, we'd never even seen Barnaby. We didn't know where to find him. The money had had to be addressed post-what-do-you-call-it at Shrewsbury. But Rupert managed to pump a girl he knows at the telephone exchange here. She found out where Barnaby had made some calls to Joan Carobleat. It was a public kiosk and we guessed he must live nearby.

'Rupert got hold of a map and I agreed to take him over in the van. I thought the idea was to find

Barnaby and to frighten him into letting us alone. I was in such a state I was ready to try anything.'

Bradlaw paused and shivered. 'Look, can't we go somewhere else? This place is freezing.'

Purbright stretched the arm with which he had been writing. 'It is on the bleak side,' he conceded. 'Try and hang on until the sergeant gets back, though, can you? He'll not be long.'

'It's hard to think in here, that's all,' Bradlaw grumbled. 'Still, if you say so . . .'

'Did you find Barnaby's place?'

'Oh, we found it all right. But he wasn't there. I tried to persuade Rupert to leave well alone. Instead of that, he started prowling round the place and found a window that was open a bit. He climbed in and let me in through the back door. It was then that I realized what he was up to. As I passed him, I spotted that drug case of his sticking out of his pocket. It gave me a shock, I can tell you.'

'You both went into the cottage, then?'

Bradlaw nodded. Then he looked sharply at the inspector. 'I haven't said it was a cottage, have I?'

'No; that's true,' said Purbright quietly.

Bradlaw let this pass, but his manner became perceptibly more careful. 'Rupert put the case down on a bench in the kitchen and took a syringe out of it. There were some tiny bottles there as well and he broke the top off one of them. Then he filled the syringe from it and went stalking round the place, looking into cupboards. After a bit, he came back to the kitchen table and squirted what was in the syringe into some milk that was standing there. "That'll have to do," he said, and I said, "You're not trying to poison him, are you?" and he said no, it was a drug to make Barnaby sleepy and less likely to go for us. I wasn't sure he was telling the truth, but I didn't argue.

'We went out through the front door and walked back to where we'd left the van under some trees. It was dark by then and we knew we'd be able to tell when Barnaby turned up because we'd see the lights of his car. I don't know how long we were sitting there. It was bloody cold and I tried two or three times to get Rupert to give up, but he wouldn't take any notice.

'I was just about asleep when a car passed us and drew up lower down. We waited until he'd driven in and then we followed. There was a light in the cottage and we crept round the back. Through the window we saw Barnaby walking about the kitchen and doing something with the stove. There was a saucepan on it. That seemed to make Rupert quite excited and several times he said: "He's bitten; the bastard's bitten!" After a while, we saw Barnaby pour some of what was in the saucepan into a plate and the rest into a beaker. He sat at the table with his back to us.

'About ten minutes later, he got up and went out of the kitchen. He came and went once or twice after that, but the last time he walked in he was looking queer. He kept feeling out for things and rocked about a bit. Rupert laughed when he saw, and I was afraid Barnaby would hear, but he didn't. He tried to sit down at the table again, but he seemed to miss the chair and flopped down out of sight. We went right up to the window and looked through, and he was there on the floor, flat out.'

Purbright licked his finger and flicked back another leaf of his notebook. At that moment, there was a knock at the mortuary door and the constable opened it to admit Love.

The inspector turned to him. 'You managed?' Love nodded. To Bradlaw, Purbright said: 'We might as well get this finished now, don't you think? Tell me if you'd rather carry on over at the office, though.'

'It doesn't matter,' said Bradlaw. 'There's not much more to tell. I just want you to know I wasn't to blame for what happened next. Honest to God, I wasn't.' He spoke pleadingly, but with an undertone of weariness.

'All right, Nab. Take your time.'

'We got back into the cottage the same way as before. Barnaby was lying fast asleep half under the table. The two of us picked him up and managed to carry him into the bedroom. He was a hell of a weight. We dropped him on the bed, and he opened his eyes and started grunting something to us. Then he went bang off again and began to snore.

'By that time, I was sick of the whole business. I went back into the kitchen to see if there were any things for making tea. Rupert stayed behind. He was standing at the foot of the bed, staring down at Barnaby with a sort of sideways grin. He hadn't said a word since we'd gone back inside.

'I couldn't find any tea things, so I went to the bedroom door to see what Rupert was up to. He was by the side of the bed and bending over it. He heard me and sort of half turned round. Then I saw he was holding that syringe again and I knew what he'd done.'

Bradlaw stopped. Looking up, Purbright saw him pass a hand round the back of his neck. He was staring at the coffin and breathing quickly through half-open lips. The inspector waited, saying nothing. It seemed to him that the barking of the consumptive old gas fire was growing louder, until the dismal little building could be fancied to shake in response to it.

When Bradlaw began speaking again, the words emerged tonelessly, like the recital of a medium. 'I fetched the van and Rupert and me carried him out to it and put him in the back. We drove off straight away and kept going. As soon as we got into Flax, we took the van into the yard at my place. When I opened it up, he was dead. That's all.'

The silence that followed was broken by Purbright suddenly slapping shut his notebook. He paced a few steps up and down, then wheeled on Bradlaw.

'Tell me, Nab—why was it necessary for Barnaby to be stripped before you brought him back that night?'

Bradlaw gave no sign of having heard. He walked to the gas fire and stooped to hold both hands before it.

Quite gently came Purbright's voice again. 'It was because he was going to travel back in style, wasn't it? In the coffin you'd remembered to take with you in that van of yours?'

Bradlaw remained crouched and silent, staring at the trembling cones of flame.

Once more Purbright addressed him. 'When Barnaby arrived at the cottage, how did you recognize him? How were you sure he was the man you were after and nobody else? You said you had never met him before.'

This time Bradlaw gave an answer, but sullenly and without turning his head. 'Rupert had seen him. You don't forget someone who's tried to stick a knife in your belly.'

'You remember what he looks like, maybe,' said Purbright. 'But it's easy to get a name wrong sometimes. I think we'd better have a second opinion, Nab.' He nodded to Love, and again the placid doorkeeper sprang to his task.

The sergeant returned almost immediately. He entered and stepped to one side of the door while the woman who had followed him stood hesitantly for a moment on the threshold. It was Joan Carobleat.

She looked from the constable to Purbright, glanced at the squatting figure of Bradlaw, and then stiffened as her eyes fell on the coffin. She turned to throw a half-smoked cigarette into the yard before coming far enough into the room for the constable to close the door behind her.

'A little party, inspector?'

She gave Purbright, who had placed himself between her and the occupied slab, a nervous, derisory smile.

'I took the liberty of asking you to come here, Mrs Carobleat, in the hope that you would be able to help us in a formal matter of identification. These things are always a little disturbing, but I promise there's nothing here to frighten or revolt you.' He took her arm and drew her gently forward.

Tense now, pale and wide-eyed, the woman allowed herself to be led towards the long, darkly gleaming box that seemed to hover monstrously, unsupported, amidst the insubstantial whiteness of the place.

They were within five or six feet of it when she suddenly stopped. Purbright felt through her arm a great rising shudder. Then another. He looked at her face. The jaw hung open and a deep rasping sigh seemed to be held there in her throat. Seconds passed. Then the sound escaped like a frothing rush of blood. It formed a single, agonizingly expelled word.

Love jumped forward to help Purbright hold the woman as she collapsed. They lowered her gently to the floor.

When she had been carried from the mortuary by Love and the constable, Purbright turned to Bradlaw.

'I thought you might have been wrong about the name,' he said. 'If this is John Barnaby, why should Mrs Carobleat have called him Harold?'

CHAPTER TWENTY-ONE

'So the late Harold Carobleat was much later than we thought,' said Mr Chubb. He permitted himself a wisp of a smile in celebration of the jest.

'He was a very astute gentleman, sir.' Purbright, from an armchair in the Chief Constable's drawing-room, stared absently at the yellow-haired Venus and listened to the faint music of crockery that came from whatever domestic retreat Mrs Chubb enjoyed.

He had just related how, six months before, increasingly importunate police inquiries into the affairs of Carobleat and Spades had driven the broker and his friends to devise evasive action. Of how, according to a second long statement by Bradlaw, this had taken the ingenious form of the supposed illness and sudden death of the principal, his secret removal to a rural retreat in Shropshire, and the burial of his firm's books and other incriminating trifles within the coffin that Bradlaw caused to be carried, in ballast, from the house of mourning. And of how Carobleat had lain low while growing the beard that was later to persuade Mrs Poole that the dead not only walk but lack razors beyond the grave.

At this point, there was a gentle tap on the door and Mrs Chubb, a fluffy, solicitous woman whom childlessness had rendered super-motherly towards all her husband's 'young men', entered with two cups of tea. She beamed at Purbright, fleetingly surveyed the windows to ensure that he was not being exposed to a draught, and departed.

The inspector sipped his tea. 'Carobleat must have fancied his position to be extremely strong,' he resumed. 'He'd avoided certain ruin and a likely spell of imprisonment. His wife went on supplying him with his share of the proceeds from the one branch of his enterprise that continued to flourish, post-humously, as it were. And he had a firm hold—or so he thought—over the associates he'd left behind, none of whom would be likely to risk exposure. He could rely on his wife watching them and also conducting a rearguard action against the inquisitive police while she wore black for the man with whom she spent every other weekend over in Shropshire.

'Incidentally, Carobleat must have been highly amused by the falling into his wife's lap of the size-able lump of insurance he'd had the foresight to provide for when the idea of 'dying' first occurred to him.

'Then something happened that he hadn't bargained for.

'He had quite a lot of money standing to his credit, and he'd naturally made arrangements to recover as much of it as he could. He had probably lodged with Gloss a simple will whereby the poor little widow would inherit the lot—less duty, that couldn't be helped—and hang on to it, together with the insurance, until it was safe for the pair to re-unite in Bermuda or somewhere.

'But up turns a will of a very different kind. To everyone's surprise, the late Mr Carobleat proves to have made over all his possessions to his good friend and neighbour, Mr Gwill. Never mind if the will is a forgery. Carobleat's wife can't do anything. And Carobleat himself is scarcely the best person to contest it.

So Gwill cleans him out, doubtless having agreed to split with the others later on.'

Chubb shook his head gravely. 'It's a damnably unethical business, Mr Purbright. I find it almost incredible that professional men could have taken part in a conspiracy of that kind.'

'Anyway,' Purbright went on, 'it proved a more dangerous adventure than they'd imagined. They'd underestimated Carobleat hopelessly. He was an exceedingly resourceful man and an unforgiving one. And he had that enormous advantage of being officially non-existent. It was as good as a cloak of invisibility.

'I think we can take it that he'd been back to Flaxborough at odd times during the past six months. He'd bought himself a new car, probably through his wife, and although an accident involving a request for his licence would have been awkward, there wouldn't have been much risk provided he came and went during darkness It seems he even got in touch with Gwill once or twice by going between the two back gardens. That would account for poor old Mrs Poole's obsession with walking corpses. What he would really be after, I fancy, was assurance that no double-crossing was being contemplated.

'Eventually, he must have learned the truth. The others couldn't stall for ever. Once he knew what was going on, he wasted no time.

'He first avoided the danger of his wife being suspected later on by getting her to spend the week-end at the inn near his cottage. He drove overnight to Flaxborough, let himself into his old house, and fixed up the cable he'd brought with him. It so happened that Mrs Poole actually saw him running the wire along the hedge, but luckily for him her wits were in no fit state to grasp what it meant.

'While he was biding his time in the house, he rang

round to Hillyard, Gwill, Bradlaw and Gloss and asked them to meet him in Gwill's house late that night. According to Bradlaw's statement, Carobleat asked for what he called a "friendly settlement" that would include his getting out of the country. They talked it over among themselves and agreed to meet him. Bradlaw says that Hillyard was then in favour of killing Carobleat quietly and burying him in the garden, but the others shied at the idea because the ground would be hard.

'Bradlaw deliberately arrived late for the meeting. He hoped that if there were trouble he would be in nice time to miss it. On the other hand, he wasn't going to stay away altogether'—Purbright consulted one of the sheets he had taken from his case—'and "risk being let down by those twisters" as he put it. Bradlaw is something of a self-made man, sir; not very articulate, but shrewd,' explained the inspector.

'I'm interested to know how Gwill was lured out on his own,' said the Chief Constable. 'He also was a shrewd fellow, as I remember.'

'He wasn't lured out on his own, sir. The other three were with him. All Carobleat had needed to do after sluicing his neighbour's drive to earth the victim nicely (it wasn't Gwill at the gate when Wilkinson's witness cycled by—he just assumed it was) was to switch on the power and make a phone call to next door.

'He said he'd hurt his leg and would be obliged if his friends would come round. They had no reason to refuse, so off they went. It was pure chance that Gwill reached the gate first. According to Bradlaw, he "jumped like a rabbit full of buckshot and went slap down on the gravel." He goes on: "We all thought he'd been shot, although we had heard nothing. I opened the gate and there was nobody there . . ." '

'He opened the gate!' exclaimed Chubb. 'Bradlaw, you mean?'

'Yes, sir. The discharge through Gwill must have blown the fuses in Carobleat's house. Anyway, this is how Bradlaw's statement goes on:

' "The three of us picked Marcus up and carried him back into the house. Rupert Hillyard took a good look at him and said he was dead. He said he thought he had been electrocuted. We agreed it might look bad for us, so we decided to put the body over in the field opposite. Roddy Gloss pulled the gate open with a walking stick in case it was still alive. We put the body in the field. I think it was Roddy's idea to lay it under the pylon to make it look like an accident. While we were still in the field, a car came out of Carobleat's place and shot off up the road. It must have been him." '

'Upon my soul!' said Chubb.

He stared for a while into his empty cup. 'Tell me, though—why did Bradwell tell you that rigmarole about Barnum—Barnaby—whatever his name was?'

Purbright shrugged and smiled. 'A forlorn effort to save what was left of his professional reputation, I believe, sir. Always at the back of poor old Bradlaw's mind was the thought of that fearfully unethical funeral trick he'd played last summer. Keeping that quiet seemed more important to him than anything else. It even blinded him to the absurdity of his story about a blackmailer who tried to kill off his benefactors.'

'Yes,' said Chubb, 'that would have been rather foolish, wouldn't it?'

Purbright levered himself out of his chair. 'If there's nothing else, sir . . .'

The door opened a little way and Mrs Chubb's rubicund face appeared. 'I think,' she said directly to

Purbright, 'that there may be one cup left in the pot, Mr er . . .'

The inspector raised his hand with the polite dignity of a man declining an earldom. 'No, ma'am, really. But thank you all the same.' He began pushing papers into his briefcase.

Mrs Chubb's smile faded. 'It's very cold outside,' she said.

Purbright felt vaguely that he had failed to discharge some sort of obligation. He swallowed and sought a suitable platitude with which Mrs Chubb might be recompensed.

Seizing on the first that came to mind, 'A very nice old table,' he murmured, appreciatively stroking the elaborate and hideous graving of its brass top.

Reaction was unexpected. 'You shall have it, Mr er . . .' Mrs Chubb instantly and warmly proclaimed.

'Oh, no . . . really . . .'

'We insist.' She looked imperiously at her husband. 'Don't we, Harcourt?'

Mr Chubb made a vague noise suggestive of assent.

'As a matter of fact,' his wife continued pleasantly, 'we aren't all that fond of it ourselves—polishing brass isn't my idea of pleasure—so Mr Chubb has been after a replacement. There was one he went to see the other week, but he left it until rather late in the evening and it had gone. It sounded awfully attractive in the advert.—Japanese ebony, or something, I think it was—do you remember, Harcourt?'

Mr Chubb stared gravely at his nails, then at the ceiling. 'Sorry, my dear . . . it's gone clean out of my head.'

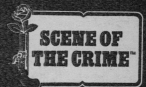